Emily Forbes is an award-winning author of Medical Romance for Mills & Boon. She has written over 25 books and has twice been a finalist in the Australian Romantic Book of the Year Award, which she won in 2013 for her novel *Sydney Harbour Hospital: Bella's Wishlist*. You can get in touch with Emily at emilyforbes@internode.on.net, or visit her website at emily-forbesauthor.com.

Also by Emily Forbes

A Kiss to Melt Her Heart
His Little Christmas Miracle
A Love Against All Odds
Falling for the Single Dad
Waking Up to Dr Gorgeous

Tempted & Tamed miniseries

A Doctor by Day…
Tamed by the Renegade
A Mother to Make a Family

Discover more at millsandboon.co.uk.

ONE NIGHT THAT CHANGED HER LIFE

BY
EMILY FORBES

MILLS & BOON

First published in Great Britain 2017
by Mills & Boon, an imprint of HarperCollins*Publishers*
1 London Bridge Street, London, SE1 9GF

Large Print edition 2018

ISBN: 978-0-263-07262-4

MIX
Paper from
responsible sources
FSC C007454

This book is produced from independently certified FSC™ paper to ensure responsible forest management. For more information visit www.harpercollins.co.uk/green.

Printed and bound in Great Britain
by CPI Group (UK) Ltd, Croydon, CR0 4YY

For Felicity.

Thank you for your love and support.
It means so much to me that you read
and enjoy my stories! This one is for you. xx

Wishing you a very Happy Birthday!

With all my love,
your goddaughter,
Emily

CHAPTER ONE

BRIGHDE HID BEHIND a conference banner as she stabbed her finger at the screen of her phone. Her hand was shaking as she tried to end the call and it took her two attempts to press the right spot. She took a deep breath, fighting to remember her yoga breathing as she fought back the tears that threatened to spill from her eyes.

She was happy for Nick, really she was, but her brother's phone call had confirmed her worst fears.

Good news for him could only mean bad news for her.

She struggled with the clasp of her bag, eventually managing to open it, and shoved her phone inside before snapping the clasp shut. She needed a drink. A strong one.

There were plenty of free drinks on offer in

the hotel ballroom where one of the major pharmaceutical drug companies was hosting the end of conference party but Brighde didn't feel like going back into the crowd. She needed space almost as much as she needed a drink.

The ballroom was on the hotel's mezzanine floor but on the floor below she knew there was a bar adjoining the lobby. She looked at the staircase; the expanse of carpet between her and the stairs looked immense and she wasn't sure if she'd make it. Her knees wobbled as she took the first step and she focused on putting one foot in front of the other until she could reach for the banister. She clutched it tightly, steadying herself for the descent. The simple task of negotiating a staircase suddenly seemed to require enormous effort. Was that a sign? She knew difficulty with motor skills was often one of the first obvious symptoms of the disease, impaired voluntary movements like gait and balance were hard to ignore, but surely that would be too much of a coincidence.

Get a hold of yourself, Brighde, she admonished herself. *You're only twenty-eight—you're not about to fall apart yet.*

She hoped she was right but it was hard to discount the feeling of mounting panic. Her chest was tight and she was finding it hard to breathe. She was surprised by her reaction to Nick's phone call. She'd always suspected that she would be dealt the bad hand and she hadn't expected to be so shocked.

This was what she'd always dreaded. It wasn't exactly a surprise but, at the end of the day, it obviously didn't matter how prepared she thought she was; the truth of it was no one wanted to know they were going to an early grave.

Somehow she managed to get down the stairs and into the bar on her wobbly legs without taking a tumble. She perched on a stool and ordered a vodka Martini. She had no idea if she liked Martinis—she drank vodka—but she felt she needed something more potent. Something that would numb the pain and a Martini sounded like it might do the trick. She didn't want to ask the bartender for suggestions; she just wanted to anaesthetise herself.

She plucked the olive from the toothpick as she drained her glass.

Martinis weren't too bad, she decided as she ordered another.

'Brighde! What are you doing down here?'

Brighde turned at the sound of her name and found Sarah, her best friend, colleague and roommate all rolled into one, making a bee-line for her across the room.

'Just collecting my thoughts.'

'Looks like you're collecting more than thoughts,' Sarah said as the bartender put a fresh cocktail on the bar.

Sarah was watching her closely as she pulled out another bar stool and sat down.

'Who was on the phone?' she asked. She'd been standing next to Brighde when she'd taken the call.

'Nick.'

'Is everything okay?'

'He got his test results back.'

'At nine o'clock at night?'

Brighde shook her head. 'No. But it took him a while to figure out how to tell me.'

'Was it bad news?'

'Not for him.' Sarah and Brighde had been friends for ten years since meeting at university, where they'd both studied nursing. Brighde had no secrets from Sarah. 'He had ten repeats.'

'He tested negative?'

Brighde nodded.

'That's great news.'

'Yes. It is,' she said, fighting to speak past the lump in her throat. She still felt like crying, even though nothing she'd heard in the phone call should make any difference. Nothing had really changed. She had her reasons for not getting tested and those reasons hadn't altered. She could go on just as before. Nick's results didn't affect her future plans but she knew they solidified her fears. His results didn't confirm her suspicions but they definitely strengthened them.

'You don't seem happy,' Sarah said.

'We each had a fifty-fifty chance of inheriting a faulty gene. There's only two of us,' Brighde explained. 'What do *you* think the chances are of both of us dodging a bullet?'

'You know the answer to that. It's still fifty-fifty. Just because Nick is clear doesn't mean you won't be. The chance of you inheriting the gene or not hasn't changed. Nick's results have no bearing on you.'

Brighde knew Sarah's facts were correct. The reality was her chances of inheriting the mutated gene hadn't changed but she still felt the odds were not in her favour. She'd always felt that. Which was why she never intended to get tested. Who wanted to know that they were going to die young? Who wanted that fear confirmed?

Not her.

'I know you're right. In theory. But I've always felt that I was going to draw the short straw and knowing Nick is okay just reinforces all those feelings. Huntington's Disease is dominantly inherited and I can't believe we'd both dodge the bullet. I don't think we could both be that lucky.'

'And I don't think there's anything you can do about it tonight,' Sarah said as she shook her head at the bartender, who was clearing Brighde's glass and asking if she wanted another. 'Come and dance, have some fun. The band's playing some good music—dancing will take your mind off it.'

Brighde let Sarah convince her to vacate the bar in favour of the dance floor. She didn't really feel like dancing but she felt less like going back to the hotel room and staring at the walls. She was feeling miserable enough already.

Xavier nursed his beer as he watched the dance floor. It was taking him a little while to get back into beer drinking. He hadn't realised he'd acquired such a taste for whisky in his years of living in Scotland, but when in Rome… Or Edinburgh.

What he was getting accustomed to far more quickly was the plethora of attractive young women at the conference. The band had been playing for some time and the dance floor was full. His eyes were drawn to a petite blonde in a sapphire dress. He'd been watching her for a while now; she'd been late onto the dance floor but even among the crowd she'd stood out. He'd tried to look elsewhere but his gaze continued to return to her. He believed you could tell exactly what a woman was like in bed by the way she moved on the dance floor. The blonde had rhythm and energy. Her dress shimmered under the lights and her hair shone, contrasting brightly against all the black outfits in the room. She was striking to look at. She wasn't smiling, she looked focused, but she danced as if she enjoyed it and he'd put money on her enjoying sex too. She looked fit and flexible and carefree, all admirable traits in his opinion, and he was hooked.

He waited until she left the dance floor. He wasn't going anywhere until he'd spoken to her. He could dance, but he wasn't about to dance in front of hundreds of his fellow medicos. He'd rather dance *à deux* and so he waited.

The band were playing a love song that was impossible to dance to without a partner. She needed pop music. Something she could lose herself in. She gestured to Sarah—she was going to grab a drink—and made her way to the bar at the side of the ballroom.

She had intended to get a water—dancing had taken her mind off the earlier phone call—but once she stopped dancing and reached the bar all her doubts returned. She'd have a water later. She needed another drink to numb the pain.

'Can I buy you a drink?'

Brighde's skin tingled as she felt, rather than saw, someone behind her. His voice was deep and quiet and although she couldn't see him she knew he was addressing her. She closed her eyes, imagining a face to go with the voice, before she turned around, hoping she wasn't going to be disappointed.

She wasn't.

She turned to find the most gorgeous man she'd seen in a long time at her side. How had she not noticed him in the room? Okay, there were hundreds of people at the conference but seriously, he was magnificent. She must have been more distracted than she'd realised.

He watched her as he waited for her answer. His dark eyes studied her, captivating her with his gaze.

'The drinks are free, you know,' she replied.

'In that case, I'll get you two.' He grinned at her, lightening the seriousness of his dark stare, and Brighde lost the last remnants of her composure.

He looked like European royalty. No, he wasn't clean-cut enough for royalty. His dark hair was slightly too long, exploding around his oval face into soft curls that just begged her to reach out and touch them. His jaw was covered in designer stubble, his eyes were dark and his forehead was strong. He was dark and swarthy and sexy as hell. Confidence oozed from him. He was impeccably dressed—his dark navy suit hung from his shoulders and fitted his frame, the pants were slim, encasing powerful thighs. He looked like a European polo player. Something out of a Jilly Cooper novel. He looked rich and successful, although of course she had no idea if that was the case, and he wanted to buy her a drink. If there was a downside to his offer she couldn't think of one.

'What are you having?' he asked. He didn't wait for her to accept his offer. He just assumed she wouldn't refuse. Was that confidence or was it simply an assumption based on the fact it was an open bar? She didn't know but she also didn't care. She wasn't going anywhere. Not now.

She shouldn't mix her drinks but the bar wasn't offering Martinis and she knew she needed more than water if she was going to be brave enough to keep up her side of the conversation with this gorgeous man. 'I'll have a white wine,' she said as she perched on a bar stool. She didn't need to sit down but she needed to take a step back. He was standing close to her; that wasn't a problem but she wanted to get a good second look at him and she needed a bit of distance to do that.

He ordered and handed her a glass. His fingers brushed hers and a spark arced between them, setting her already nervous heart racing. It had been several months since she'd shared a drink with a man but she knew it wasn't the length of time making her react this way.

Was the touch accidental? she wondered as he tapped his beer glass against her wine and made a toast. 'To new experiences.'

He held her gaze a fraction longer than was polite and her stomach flipped and she knew his touch had been deliberate. Her body was responding to him in a way it never had before. She'd never felt such immediate attraction or, if she was honest, such blatant lust before. He made her think of naked bodies and tangled sheets and raw, amazing sex and she knew exactly how this night would end. 'Indeed,' she replied as a sense of delicious anticipation flooded through her. She smiled and added, 'I'm Brighde.'

'Xavier.'

She didn't need to know any more than that.

'Have you enjoyed the conference?' he asked her.

So he was part of the conference and hadn't just snuck in for the free drinks.

'It's been really good,' she said as she put her glass on the bar and crossed her legs, pleased that she'd had a little bit of free time to lie by the hotel pool and work on her tan. 'But I could do with a few days off to recover before I go back to work. I'm heading home tomorrow, back to work on Monday.'

'That's a pity. I'll be here for a few more days.'

'Work or pleasure?' she asked.

'Purely pleasure.' He kept his dark eyes fixed on her as he reached past her shoulder, picking up a napkin from the bar. His arm brushed against her skin and she could feel his words on her cheek, soft little puffs of air. She knew he didn't need the napkin, she knew it had just been an excuse to lean in but she wasn't complaining. She could feel the electricity surging between them. They could power the room with the heat that was being generated between them. She wasn't aware of the music, the dancing, of anything that was going on around them. She was lost in the sensation he was evoking in her. She could feel his charisma wrapping itself around her as his pheromones enveloped her. Her nipples hardened and she squirmed in her seat. She pressed her thighs together as heat pooled low in her belly.

'I've been working in Scotland,' he told her, 'but the conference seemed like a good way to keep the taxman happy and visit my family.'

'Family?'

'My parents live here.'

'You're travelling alone? No partner? No wife?' She played with the ends of her hair, feigning casualness. She had to know the answer. She had rules and standards. She knew she would have sex with this gorgeous stranger—having sex would be a far healthier, and much more entertaining, distraction than drowning her worries with alcohol—but first she needed to establish some ground rules. She didn't want to make any mistakes.

'No wife. No girlfriend. No significant other.'

Now it was her turn to smile. 'Good to know.' She kept her gaze fixed on him now, wanting him to know where she stood. What she wanted. She didn't need to know anything else about him. She knew she wouldn't see him again. He was only visiting; she was leaving tomorrow. She hadn't had sex for ages and a one-night stand with this gorgeous man was a good option all round. No commitment, just a bit of fun and a good way to keep her mind busy. She didn't want time to think about her brother's phone call. She wanted something to take her mind off her situation. This was perfect.

She wanted Xavier.

And she wanted him to know that.

But Xavier was looking to his right.

Sarah had joined them.

Brighde watched her friend looking from her to Xavier and she knew she was taking in the distance, or lack of, between them. She watched as Sarah, quite blatantly, checked him out.

'I'm off,' Sarah said when she'd finished her inspection. 'Are you coming?'

Brighde thought about it for a second—okay, to be honest, a millisecond—she didn't need any longer than that when Xavier was looking at her with his come-to-bed eyes. 'No, I think I'm going to stay here for a bit.'

She knew Sarah's question had been rhetorical. She knew her plans for the rest of the evening were written all over her face but she didn't care. She wasn't even looking at Sarah as she answered; she couldn't make herself tear her eyes away from Xavier. He oozed sex appeal and she knew it was only a matter of time before she would be in his bed. She could feel it. She knew he wanted it too. She could feel the desire coming off him in waves and he was just what she needed. Taking a gorgeous man to bed ticked all the right boxes and it was a habit she had no intention of breaking. Okay, so she didn't do it all that often—she could barely remember the last time she'd even had sex—but a one-night stand was the perfect way to scratch an itch.

She needed sex but she didn't need a relationship. One night was enough. There was no need to go into details, no need to reveal anything personal about herself. She didn't consider sex to be personal—sex with a stranger couldn't hurt her, not as much as revealing her fears. She could happily share her body but not her mind. Her body was going to let her down one day; she owed it nothing.

Sarah nodded and smiled. She lent forwards and kissed Brighde's cheek. 'Have fun,' she whispered into Brighde's ear.

Brighde watched her go and when she turned back to Xavier she found he'd moved closer to her. His thigh pressed against her knee. She shifted forward on the bar stool, sliding her knee against the inside of his thigh. Their intentions were perfectly clear.

She looked up at him to find his dark eyes watching her. Her reaction was immediate and primal and she could feel her nipples jutting against the cool silk of her dress. She saw his gaze drop lower, saw him take in the peak of her nipples against the fabric of her dress. When he looked back at her his gaze was so intense and full of heat she thought she might melt into a pool of desire at his feet.

'Can I offer you a nightcap upstairs?' he asked as he lifted her glass from her hand. He reached across her to put her half-finished drink on the bar and the back of his hand brushed across her chest, grazing her nipple. Brighde felt as if she might climax on the spot.

She swallowed and nodded as she licked her lips. Despite everything she'd had to drink her throat was suddenly dry and she was having difficulty breathing, let alone speaking. She was experienced in the art of seduction but not in relationships. She didn't communicate with words. She sought the comfort of sex when she needed it, emotionally or physically. Tonight she needed it to distract herself. It had worked in the past and, looking at Xavier, she was sure it would work again today.

He took her hand and helped her off the stool. Once again her legs had turned to jelly but she barely noticed this time. She was too aware of the tingling in her belly and the intense weight of expectation and excitement in her groin.

Xavier held the door for her as she stepped into the lift. The lift had four other occupants and Brighde stood slightly apart from Xavier. She needed to keep some distance, otherwise she was in danger of throwing herself at him in front of a crowd. He pushed the button for the sixteenth floor while she leant against the wall of the lift; she needed something solid to keep her upright. She wanted to lean against Xavier but didn't dare while they had company. She didn't trust herself to maintain a sense of decency.

'What floor would you like?' one of the other passengers asked her.

'Sixteen,' she replied as she tried to avoid eye contact with Xavier, the gorgeous stranger.

Over the heads and shoulders of the other people sharing their lift she was totally aware of him. The man exuded sex appeal. Tall, dark, handsome and well-built. His dark hair was thick and just long enough to show the wave through it. There was no grey in his hair but a hint of it lightened the tidy stubble that darkened his jaw. He was well-groomed but definitely all man and he was watching her with his dark chocolate eyes as she studied him. His eyes were slightly hooded; he reminded her of a predatory bird. She felt like a sparrow in the piercing gaze of a falcon and she knew she was firmly in his sights.

The lift stopped several times but it wasn't until the fourteenth floor, when the doors closed, that it was finally just the two of them who remained.

She continued to study him. His hands were large, as were his feet. Even his slightly hooked nose was on the generous side. Brighde was twenty-eight years old and she was a midwife, she knew anatomy, and even though it was purported to be an old wives' tale she knew you could judge the size of a man's appendage by the size of his hands, feet and nose. She swallowed. She wouldn't have to wait long to test her theory.

His eyes hadn't strayed from hers and she knew he was visualising what was under her dress, just as she was imagining what she might find under his clothes. The idea gave her a rush of lust and she stepped a little closer as the lift doors eased shut.

He smelt fantastic. She was tempted to press the emergency stop button but she didn't want to be surprised by a maintenance team coming to rescue them. She could wait two more floors. Maybe.

She was aware of her breathing now. Heavy and laboured.

He reached out one hand and put it on her waist and she could feel the heat of his fingers through the thin silk fabric of her dress. He pulled her closer until she was pressed against him. She could feel his desire now, a thick, hard bulge pressing into her. She tipped her head back and looked up at him as the lift stopped and the doors slid open.

CHAPTER TWO

SHE LEANT AGAINST HIM, not trusting her legs to support her, as he led her to his room. He swiped the electronic key card over the door and held it open for her.

The room was a carbon copy of hers, with the exception of the bed. She was sharing with Sarah so their room had twin beds. Xavier had a room to himself, and a king-size bed that she intended to put to good use dominated the space.

She stepped inside and somehow managed to wait until he stepped in behind her and closed the door. She turned around and his mouth was instantly on hers. His hands at her back.

She wasn't interested in talking. She didn't want to know anything about him. She didn't *need* to know anything about him. His voice was deep and velvety smooth and it did funny things to her insides but she didn't need to hear it.

She parted her lips and his tongue delved deeper, exploring her, tasting her.

She pulled his shirt free from his trousers and undid the buttons, running her hands over his chest. The muscles were firm and warm under her fingers and dark hair covered his skin.

She could feel wetness pooling between her thighs. She pressed against him, wanting to feel the thickness of his erection, knowing she wouldn't be disappointed.

She closed her eyes and the room started to spin. Just a little, just enough for her to recognise she'd had more to drink than she'd realised. Drunk and emotional. That wasn't a good combination. But she wasn't so drunk that she didn't know exactly where she was and what she was doing, she thought as she felt his hand slide up under her dress. She opened her eyes as his hand cupped her buttock. He lifted her off her feet and continued to deepen the kiss as she wrapped her legs around his waist.

He carried her to the bed. She knelt on the edge as he opened the bedside drawer and retrieved a little foil packet. He put it on the bedside table, watching her as he let it go. His intentions were clear and Brighde knew he was asking for her acquiescence. In reply she reached up and slid his jacket and shirt from his shoulders, letting them drop to the floor. She wasn't changing her mind now.

He kicked off his shoes as she fumbled with the buckle of his belt. Finally, the belt came loose and she undid his trousers, letting him step out of them.

She swallowed as she looked at him standing before her. He pushed his boxer shorts off his hips and his erection sprang free.

He was even more impressive than she'd imagined. Thick and proud. He was glorious.

He reached for her again and she lifted her arms above her head as he whipped her dress from her body. She wasn't wearing a bra; she was as naked as he was save for her knickers and heels.

She stood up, brushing her breasts across his chest, and watched in fascination as his chocolate-brown eyes darkened further.

She spun him around, pushing him lightly backwards, making him sit on the edge of the bed. She needed to control this.

She stepped out of her underwear and put her legs either side of his, straddling his thighs.

She pushed him gently again, forcing him to lie back, as she climbed onto the bed and sat across him.

She plucked the foil packet from the bedside table and tore it open, sheathing him and protecting herself.

She was in a hurry now. Foreplay had been dealt with at the bar and in the lift. Silent communication and agreement had got them this far and she was ready and eager for the satisfaction she anticipated.

She put one hand on each side of his head and lifted her hips as he guided himself inside her, filling her. She closed her eyes as she concentrated on the sensations swamping her. The thickness of his shaft, the slight stretch of the muscles in her inner thighs as she spread her legs wider to take him deeper inside her.

She leant forwards as she raised and lowered her hips, sliding up and down his length. She opened her eyes and watched as his lips parted, listened to his sigh of pleasure. His hooded eyes were darker now, even more intense. She felt his hands on her skin and then his breath as he lifted his head and took one breast into his mouth.

Brighde moaned as waves of pleasure consumed her and her body came to life.

His hands were on her bottom and she could feel each individual finger against her skin. He wasn't controlling the pace though; his hands were just following her movements, following her rhythm and pace. She was setting the tone. She was in control.

She sat up and felt her nipple peak as the cool air replaced his warm mouth. She wanted to watch him as they made love. She wanted a chance to commit it all to memory.

She reached behind her back and down between his thighs. Her fingers searching. She cupped his balls in her hand; they were hard and tight and cool in her grasp. She rolled them in her hand before circling his shaft with her fingers, following its movement to feel it disappear inside her. Deep inside her.

Her knees were shaking but the muscles in her buttocks and between her thighs were tight. She was panting quickly now, her breath coming in short, shallow gasps almost as if she were forgetting to breathe. She didn't have enough muscle control spare to focus on breathing.

She couldn't wait much longer. She could feel the waves of an orgasm threatening to break over her.

His hands had moved to her hips now, keeping her in place. Not that she had any plans to go anywhere. Maybe he was just holding her up.

She could barely keep her eyes open. Every cell in her body was focused on pleasure and there was nothing left for the basics. Nothing left to spare on breathing or thinking.

Brighde let herself go, giving in to the burst of light that wanted to explode in her.

'Now,' she begged and she felt him shudder and heard herself cry out as they climaxed together.

She collapsed, exhausted, spent and fulfilled onto his chest.

He wrapped his arms around her and she felt him kiss the top of her head. She closed her eyes and breathed deeply, inhaling his scent. She'd had a few one-night stands—she considered them her only practical option as she wasn't willing to risk having a real relationship—but she couldn't say she'd ever found them terribly satisfying and she definitely couldn't ever remember one as immensely gratifying as tonight.

She wouldn't mind repeating it, but that wasn't in her rule book.

One night only. With single men. And only with men she knew she wouldn't bump into at work or in the supermarket.

But Xavier was on holiday from Scotland.

Maybe she could stretch it to twice. But she was leaving tomorrow. Going back to Melbourne and back to work. She only had one night so she'd have to take her second chance tonight and surely twice in one night didn't count.

She lay with her head on his chest and her fingers splayed across his stomach and listened to the rhythm of his heartbeat under her ear. She closed her eyes and let the silence drift over her.

She woke an hour later. The hotel room curtains were open and the city lights lit up the room. Xavier's arm was draped over her shoulder and she slid out from under it, careful not to disturb him. She needed to go.

She ducked, naked, into the bathroom but when she returned to collect her clothes he was awake. He was lying on his back watching her. The covers were off and he made no attempt to hide the fact that he was ready and willing to make love again.

Brighde forgot all about getting dressed as she let him pull her back into bed.

But this time she took care not to fall asleep afterwards. She waited until he drifted off before she dressed and snuck out in the early hours of the morning.

There was no exchange of phone numbers or even last names. She didn't know anything about him and that was the way she wanted it. She would never see him again. She felt a tiny twinge of disappointment but even though he was magnificent she wasn't about to break her own rule.

She didn't do weekends. She didn't do relationships.

One night was enough.

There was no danger of falling in love in only one night.

Brighde changed into scrubs ready for another night shift. Her fifth straight. She was exhausted; the maternity wing had been really busy. That wasn't unusual; Parkville Private Hospital had the largest private maternity service in Melbourne and they were always busy, but the past few shifts had been ridiculous. The nurses were blaming the full moon; there was no scientific evidence to back up their suspicions but years of experience had taught them that a full moon seemed to trigger labour, not only in the women who had reached full term but also for those who were overdue as well as for plenty who were a week or two away from their due dates. The department was bursting at the seams and Brighde was looking forward to a few days off at the end of this shift. Only eight hours to go.

She tied the laces on her sneakers and headed for handover, hoping that tonight would be quiet.

'Brighde, you can take over from Jacqui. She's got delivery room three.' The charge nurse distributed the patients among the new staff.

'I've got Kirsty Jones,' Jacqui told her.

Brighde remembered Kirsty from prenatal appointments. 'First baby, husband is Matt, right?' she clarified.

Jacqui nodded. 'She's been in labour for about

twelve hours and in active phase for a few hours now. Seven centimetres dilated, contractions four minutes apart. She probably hasn't got long to go. Do you want me to stay until she delivers?'

It was common for the midwives to extend their shifts if they thought their patients were close to delivering. It made for good continuity of care and the mums appreciated having one midwife throughout. But it wasn't always possible. Lots of babies took far longer than one shift to make their appearance.

'Is there much else happening at the moment?' Brighde asked, meaning, *Are we likely to be run off our feet?*

'No.'

'Go home, then,' she told Jacqui. 'I know Kirsty. I've got this.'

'Thanks. I've called her doctor. He's on his way. Dr Davey is on holidays and Dr O'Donnell, the new OB/GYN is covering for him.' Jacqui was already untying her ponytail, getting ready to leave, as she gave Brighde the final information.

'OK, all good.'

'Kirsty, how are you?' Brighde stepped into delivery room three and greeted Kirsty and her husband. Kirsty looked tired and Matt didn't look as if he was faring much better. 'We've had a shift change, it's my turn now but you won't have any more changes after this. I promise I'll be here when your baby is born.'

'You'd better be,' Kirsty panted. 'Your shifts are eight hours, right? If this baby isn't out by then, I'm leaving.'

Brighde smiled.

'What?' Kirsty asked.

'We hear that a lot at this stage, when you've had enough, that's when we know you're getting close.'

Kirsty grimaced as she was gripped by another contraction.

'How are you doing, Matt?' Brighde asked as she waited for Kirsty's contraction to ease.

This stage was hard on the partners; she knew he'd be feeling useless.

'I'm okay but isn't there anything to do to speed this up?' he asked.

'Sorry, not at this point. She's very close. We've just got to let things take their course. Natural is best.'

Jacqui had attached a monitor to Kirsty's abdomen to record the contractions and Brighde checked the readout. The contractions were now two minutes apart, lasting for around sixty seconds and getting stronger.

'I'm just going to take a look to see how your labour is progressing,' Brighde said as she pulled a pair of gloves on.

'Eight centimetres. You're getting there,' she said. 'You're in the transition phase now. It won't be much longer.'

'We haven't even seen the doctor,' Matt said.

'He's on his way. There's nothing for him to do yet. Trust me, you don't want the doctor in early. If things are going well you don't need him until the end.'

Kirsty's labour seemed to be progressing as expected and Brighde thought they wouldn't really need the doctor at all but she also knew that at Parkville Private the patients paid for, and expected to see, the doctor.

Kirsty cried out as another contraction took over. She was getting restless. 'God, it hurts.'

'If you think you can manage to get onto all fours that might ease the pressure on your back,' Brighde told her. 'Matt, you could run a flannel under hot water and give Kirsty's back a rub.' That would hopefully distract Kirsty, ease her discomfort and give Matt something useful to do. 'You'll meet your baby soon.'

Matt had followed her suggestion and returned from the en suite bathroom with a warm flannel. Brighde let him look after Kirsty while she checked the equipment, making sure she had everything she needed for the delivery at arm's reach. As she worked she listened to Matt as he tried to reassure Kirsty. She could hear the love and affection in his voice, along with concern, and it made her wish that she had someone to share her life with. Someone who would love and support her. But she knew that would be asking a lot. She'd vowed long ago that she wouldn't put someone through what she'd been through. She'd made a pact with herself that she would stay single. She wanted to be loved but she wouldn't risk it.

Thinking about being in love led her to thinking about her brother. After all the pledges they'd made, the promise not to get tested, Nick had fallen in love with Imogen and everything had changed. The pact she and Nick had made years before, agreeing not to have genetic testing, had ended when Nick had fallen in love. He wanted to start a family and he needed answers. Brighde couldn't blame him for that. But now she knew her decision to stay single and free was justified. She had watched her mother's life disintegrate and she'd vowed not to put herself or loved ones in that same position. Which meant not allowing herself to fall in love. That was the only way to avoid the heartache. To avoid the risk. She had to stick to her plan. As much as she'd like to share her life with someone, she couldn't commit to anything more than one night.

The last night she'd spent with someone had been with Xavier. She wondered how he was. Whether he was back in Scotland. Whether he ever thought about her. She couldn't deny she'd been thinking about him. A lot. In the maternity suites she'd found herself comparing all the partners to Xavier. Wondering what he would be like in the same situation. Would he be the bossy, know-it-all expectant father who'd read all the books? Or would he be the kind, gentle, supportive partner who was only concerned about his wife. Not that it mattered. Her silent imaginings were a waste of time. Xavier was gone.

She had to stick to her plan and even if she wanted to change her mind Xavier wasn't around. That boat had sailed. That was why she'd let her hormones carry her away that night. Because she'd known she'd never see him again. But she hadn't been able to get him out of her head, despite the fact that the night she'd spent with him was now almost eight weeks ago. She really needed to get him out of her system.

She'd expected the sex to be good—the sparks she'd felt between them had been too huge to ignore—but she hadn't expected it to be the best sex of her life. But that didn't mean she couldn't have better. Xavier might have become her new benchmark but that didn't mean someone else out there couldn't match up or even improve on him.

Maybe that was the answer. Maybe she just needed to have sex with someone else. She needed to erase the memory of him. Something about Xavier had got under her skin but she couldn't afford to get fixated on someone she'd never see again. That had been the whole point. Anonymous sex was the only way to go. She didn't get involved. She didn't do relationships and she really didn't have time to spend thinking about him. She needed to get this baby delivered, and however many others decided to be born tonight, and then she'd go home, get a good eight hours sleep and tomorrow she'd start to wipe all traces of Xavier from her mind. She'd go back to the old, independent Brighde. She didn't need a man; she was fine.

She didn't *want* a man she told herself as she prepared to check Kirsty's progress again.

She was now nine centimetres dilated and Brighde could see the baby's head. She wondered how far away the doctor was. If he wasn't already here he was likely to miss the delivery altogether.

'Almost there, Kirsty. You're doing really well. Not long now.' She stood and pulled off her gloves. 'I'll fetch the doctor.'

Brighde stepped out of the delivery room and was surprised to find Sarah just outside the door. She was working a late shift too but she was working in the nursery. Maybe she was collecting a baby. But she grabbed Brighde's arm.

'Good, I'm glad I found you.'

'What's the matter?'

'There's something I need to tell you,' her

friend said as she dragged her towards the nurses' station.

'What is it?' Brighde had no idea what could be so urgent. 'I'm in the middle of a delivery.'

'I know,' Sarah said, 'but this is important. Dr O'Donnell—the doctor covering for Dr Davey—you're looking for him, aren't you?'

Brighde nodded.

'That's him.' Sarah tilted her head to her left a few times in quick succession, nodding towards the nurses' station.

Brighde frowned. 'Who is?'

'Dr O'Donnell. It's him. From the conference.'

Brighde saw the back of a head. Her eyes took in the thick, dark, slightly curly hair. The tall, broad, masculine shoulders. Her stomach flipped as recognition slapped her. He wasn't someone she knew from staff but he wasn't a complete stranger either.

He turned, maybe a sixth sense alerting him to the fact he was being scrutinised, and their eyes locked.

Brighde took a deep breath and held it. The man she'd shared the best sex of her life with was standing six feet away.

CHAPTER THREE

'OH, MY GOD.'

He wasn't supposed to be here.

Brighde turned to Sarah, dragging her eyes away from Xavier's perfect face. Her heart was racing. 'What the hell is *he* doing here?'

Sarah shrugged. 'He's the new OB/GYN.'

'Seriously?'

'Yep.'

She swore under her breath.

Be cool, Brighde, she told herself. *No one needs to know anything.*

But she had to fight the urge to turn on her heel and run out of the door.

She looked back at him. He didn't look nearly as surprised as she felt. Maybe he was just better at hiding his feelings. He nodded in her direction, a half-nod, and smiled and Brighde's heart did a little flip. How the hell was she supposed to handle this? She was always so careful to ensure that she didn't mix her private and professional lives, yet here was the man who had quite literally swept her off her feet, had seen every naked inch of her and given her the time of her life, standing in front of her expecting to work together. She'd never, ever been in this situation before.

Her flight and fight responses were having their own private battle inside her. She was very tempted to go with flight but she knew that wasn't going to give her the answers she wanted or make the problem go away. If he was, as Sarah had said, the new OB/GYN, she had to assume he was here to stay.

Maybe she could just ignore him, she thought as she half turned away, giving herself a moment to try to get her reactions under control. But she knew that was impossible. He was the doctor she was looking for. He was the one she needed to deliver Kirsty's baby. They'd be working together, which meant she wasn't going to be able to ignore him.

And now he was beside her. She knew he was. She could feel him. Ignoring him was definitely not going to be an option. Thankfully, Sarah still stood to her left, giving her moral support. She needed it.

Sarah had heard Brighde's recount of the night spent in Xavier's bed many times over the past eight weeks but Brighde had never expected the two of them to meet. She felt her cheeks redden as she thought about the intimate details she'd shared with her best friend.

'Hello, Brighde. I didn't expect to see you here.'

His deep voice washed over her and she fought the impulse to close her eyes and give in. His tone was seductive. She knew he probably didn't mean it to be but that was the effect it had on her. She glanced at Sarah, wondering if Xavier affected her the same way, but she seemed completely relaxed whereas Brighde felt as if someone had tied her up in knots while she wasn't paying attention.

Was he pleased or disappointed to see her?

She shouldn't care.

But she did.

And she couldn't ignore him. Not while he stood beside her. She turned towards him, lifted her head and willed herself to keep it together as she looked into the depths of his dark eyes.

And there it was. The same seductive come-to-bed expression that had drawn her to him the first time. Different circumstances, same reaction. She was in trouble.

Her eyes drifted lower, away from his carnal gaze, as she fought temptation. She couldn't afford to go to pieces here. She had a job to do.

He was wearing scrubs. Shapeless blue hospital scrubs that did nothing to disguise the width of his shoulders, the length of his legs and the flatness of his stomach. She could still remember how every ridge and groove of his abdominals felt under her hand. She closed her eyes briefly and when she opened them she was looking at his hand. He had his fingers wrapped around a coffee mug. She could remember when those fingers had been cupped around the cheek of her arse.

Her breath caught in her throat.

She couldn't breathe. She needed to breathe.

She looked at Sarah in desperation.

Sarah stuck out her hand. 'Hi, I'm Sarah, one of the midwives. I don't think we were ever properly introduced.'

'Nice to see you again,' Xavier replied as he took her hand.

He was all charm. He even remembered Sarah.

'Brighde is looking after your patient,' Sarah said, obviously figuring she'd given Brighde enough time to gather her wits. 'She'll take you to the delivery room.'

'Lead the way.' He was looking at her again. She was caught, spellbound, by his gaze. *Come on, get yourself together.*

Sarah gave her a gentle push, making Brighde's

feet move. She doubted she would have been able to put one foot in front of the other otherwise.

Okay. Focus, Brighde. Just do your job and worry about Dr O'Donnell and his bedroom eyes later. That's the way. Think of him as Dr O'Donnell and not Xavier. Separate him into two parts, professional and private, and just remember to keep them separate. Pretend you've never met him. He's nothing to you. And, whatever you do, don't start a personal conversation.

But she was aware of his body heat as they walked side by side down the corridor. His scent. She even imagined she could hear him breathing. And she had the feeling once again that her cells were straining towards him. She concentrated hard to make sure she kept walking in a straight line. She could feel herself veering towards him. She needed to stay on track.

She breathed deeply as she put her hand on the door to the delivery room.

Focus, Brighde.

'Our mum-to-be is Kirsty, twenty-nine years old and forty-one weeks' gestation with her first baby, so a little overdue. No complications with the pregnancy. She's been in labour for about twelve hours but just reached nine centimetres. Kirsty is tired but the baby is fine, although it's quite large. Around four kilograms. Her husband is Matt.'

Xavier pushed open the door and strode into the room, full of confidence. No one would ever imagine he was new to the hospital. He looked as if he'd been here for ever. He looked completely comfortable. *She* was the one who was unsettled.

Xavier introduced himself to Kirsty and Matt while he washed his hands. He pulled on a pair of gloves while Brighde fastened a gown over his scrubs and resisted the temptation to run her hands down his back. She stepped away as soon as she was done; the further away she could stay the better.

'Let's see what's going on, shall we?' Xavier said as he crossed to the bed.

Kirsty was still kneeling on the bed with Matt supporting her as she rocked. Brighde expected Xavier to reposition Kirsty. She expected him to ask her to lie down, as that would make it easier for him to see what was going on, but she was pleasantly surprised when he pushed a small wheeled stool over to the bed with his foot and sat behind Kirsty.

'Good news,' he said as he finished his examination. 'You're fully dilated and I can see the baby's head. Everything's good. Are you comfortable in that position?' He was calm, relaxed, friendly, engaging. He was perfect.

'No,' Kirsty half laughed as another contraction gripped her.

'Sorry, bad choice of words,' Xavier admitted. 'What I meant was, would you like to stay in this position or did you want to try something else? From my experience this is often the most comfortable position to give birth but it's up to you.'

'I don't think I can move,' Kirsty said.

'All right, stay just like you are. Are you okay, Matt?'

Matt would need to support Kirsty in that position. Kirsty was leaning on his shoulders and he had his arms wrapped around her waist. It was an awkward position for both Matt and Xavier but Xavier didn't seem fazed by it. Brighde didn't know many obstetricians who would happily make their own job more uncomfortable. Most still went for the standard, 'lie on your back, bend your knees and push'.

Brighde had to force herself to focus on the task at hand. She couldn't afford to be distracted by Xavier although it was hard when all she could see was the width of his shoulders, the dark curls on the back of his head and his long fingers as they rested on the bed. His voice alone was enough to distract her without the additional fact that he was sitting mere inches from her. Her fingers itched to reach out and slide through his hair. She stepped away to check that she had a warm blanket ready for the baby. Knowing she did but needing an activity to keep her hands busy.

But she kept one eye on him.

'Your baby is doing fine,' he said as he checked the foetal heart rate monitor before checking Kirsty again. 'When you feel the next contraction I want you to push. It's time to meet your baby.'

Brighde took up her place at Xavier's side, ready for the delivery.

'Okay, here we go. Push!' Xavier instructed. 'Stop now, breathe. Okay, nearly there, you're doing great, Kirsty. All right, you can push again.'

He delivered the baby's head before letting Kirsty rest again. The baby's shoulders would be next and Xavier had to reach and contort himself for this part due to the position he'd left Kirsty in. 'Okay, one last push. You're almost there.'

The baby slid out into Xavier's waiting hands. 'Congratulations. A healthy boy.'

Kirsty collapsed back onto her haunches and

Brighde helped her to lie down. Xavier handed the baby to his mum, laying him on her chest.

The next few minutes were busy but Brighde knew Kirsty and Matt would barely notice as Xavier gave the required injections and Brighde did the Apgar scores. They worked smoothly together and as Xavier got ready to deliver the placenta Brighde took the baby to be weighed, measured and attach the identification bands.

She loved this part of her job. She took any chance she could to hold and cuddle the babies, getting her fix, as she didn't plan to have children of her own.

'He's absolutely perfect,' Brighde said as she handed him back to Kirsty. 'I'll give you some time together,' she said once the new parents looked settled, 'and I'll be back in a little while to help you shower.'

She would attend to the rest of Kirsty's care later. For now, they just needed some time alone to get acquainted with their new arrival.

Xavier followed her out of the room, untying his apron as he walked. They threw their dirty aprons and gloves into the rubbish and stood, side by side, at the sinks to wash their hands.

Brighde's skin tingled with his proximity. She still couldn't quite believe he was here. One part of her wanted to tear off his scrubs, another wanted to scream at him and a third part of her wanted to burst into tears. She had no idea why she felt like crying. She'd been highly emotional lately but she'd been blaming the fact that her brother had found love along with her own inability to stop thinking about Xavier and now he was here, standing beside her, smiling at her, and she had no idea what she was supposed to do.

He wasn't supposed to be here and he *definitely* shouldn't be smiling at her, turning her insides to mush and her legs to jelly.

His pull on her was magnetic. It felt as if all her cells were straining towards him, giving the impression that, if it were possible, they'd leap out of her body and into his. It felt as if he could absorb her, as if she could disappear into him and all that would be left of her would be her empty skin pooled on the floor at his feet. All traces of her gone.

She'd never felt anything like this before.

All her one-night stands had been just that. One night. She'd never seen any of them again and she'd never had to think about how she would feel if she found herself in this exact situation. She certainly hadn't expected to feel such a strong attraction and her reaction frustrated her.

'What the hell are you doing here?' Her voice was quiet but her tone was anything but friendly. She was irritated with herself and annoyed with him. She didn't want to cause a scene but she had to have some answers, otherwise she knew she would go crazy. 'Why aren't you back in Scotland?'

'Because I live here now.'

What? She *never* would have slept with him if she'd known he was going to turn up on her doorstep.

'You live here?'

'Yes.'

'What about Scotland?'

'I said I'd been working in Scotland; I didn't actually say I was going back.'

Her brow creased and he knew she was trying to recall the scant conversation they'd had. They hadn't spent much time talking. She probably knew as little about him as he did about her. Although he could recall every curve of her body, the softness of her skin and the touch of her hand, he didn't know much beyond that. He hadn't needed to at the time. He hadn't even known she was a midwife. He'd assumed she worked in the health profession because she was at the conference but he hadn't given any thought to what she did for a living. He hadn't been interested in that.

But now he praised his good fortune in accepting this job at Parkville Private. Working with Brighde could turn out to be a pleasant surprise, although her tone suggested she wasn't quite as excited about the idea as he was.

'But you're not supposed to be *here*!' she said,

confirming his suspicions that she wasn't especially pleased to see him. '*Why* are you here?'

'Have dinner with me and I'll tell you.'

'No, thank you.'

'No?' He wasn't sure that he'd heard right. She was turning down his invitation. 'Really?' He couldn't remember the last time he was knocked back.

'Haven't you ever had anyone say no to you before?' she asked, but she was still frowning as if this was all very serious rather than the pleasant coincidence he saw it to be.

'Not often,' he admitted. And never straight after he'd spent the night with someone. 'So, what's your objection to dinner?'

'I didn't expect to see you again.'

'Nor I you, but that's no reason not to share a meal.'

'And I never would have slept with you if I'd known we'd be working together.'

'It's just dinner, Brighde. You can show me around Melbourne.'

'I don't think so.'

'Why not? Are you seeing someone?' That was a possibility he hadn't thought of until now but it was quite likely. The conference and the one night they'd shared was now months ago. Maybe she wasn't single any more. That wouldn't surprise him but it would definitely be a shame.

'No.' She shook her head and the golden curls that had come loose from her ponytail bobbed around her shoulders.

'Well, in that case, how can I convince you to change your mind?' He wasn't one to give up easily. And, besides, sex with Brighde had been incredible and he was more than willing to get to know her better and see if she could be persuaded to give it another go.

'You can't.'

'There's nothing I can do?'

She shook her head again. 'It's not you. It's me.'

Xavier almost laughed until he realised she wasn't kidding. 'Seriously? That old chestnut.'

What could he have done to offend her so terribly that she wouldn't share a meal with him?

'I mean it. I don't date and I don't do dinner.'

'Ever?'

'Never.'

He'd never heard anything so ridiculous. Who didn't date? Even his disastrous last relationship hadn't put him off the idea of dating. If you didn't date you were destined to spend your life alone and who wanted to do that? Not him. 'Why is that?'

'I'm happy on my own.'

'That's a very male attitude. Don't all women want a partner?'

'You don't know much about women, do you?' she countered.

'I actually thought I knew women pretty well. I have four sisters and I work as an OB/GYN. I work with women every day.' Hormonal ones too, but he thought better of mentioning that.

'Maybe so but there are always exceptions. You can't put us all in the one basket.'

So it would seem.

'I don't need a man to complete me,' she continued. 'I might need him for sex but there is more than one way to skin a cat.'

'You're very direct.' Her directness was appealing. Another tick in the box. After playing guessing games with his ex, Brighde's honesty was refreshing. But it wasn't getting him what he wanted.

'I don't see the point in playing games. Life is short; I intend to live my life by my rules. So, why didn't you go back to Scotland?'

She looked as if she'd have him on a plane right then and there if it was up to her.

'I'm Melbourne born and bred. I've come home.'

'So you don't need me to show you around Melbourne, then.'

'No.' He laughed, trying to ease the tension he could feel emanating from her. She was wound up tight. 'Guilty as charged. But I warn you, I will try again. I'd like to have dinner with you. Just dinner; we won't call it a date. No expectations, no strings.' He wasn't looking for a serious relationship but Brighde wasn't even looking at him any more.

'I need to get back to Kirsty,' she said as she dried her hands. And then she was gone. Leaving him alone and completely confused. And naturally intrigued. She'd thrown him a challenge by knocking him back and he wasn't about to retreat.

Anyone listening to her would think she was mad. *He* probably thought she was mad. But she'd prefer to risk being considered crazy than to risk falling in love. That was not on her agenda. She needed to get away. Far away. From his easy charm and his come-to-bed eyes and his to-die-for body before she made any more mistakes. She could totally understand why he wasn't often rejected. He was completely gorgeous and the sex had been fantastic but he wasn't for her. She couldn't afford to relax her rules. She didn't do second dates or dinner or whatever he wanted to call it. She couldn't accept his invitation, no matter how much she was tempted.

So she walked away, even though it was hard to do, and returned to Kirsty and her baby. She had a new mum to care for. A job to do. There was no time to think about what-ifs and to wish things were different.

She helped Kirsty to breastfeed her baby, then shower and dress. She settled her into her room and left Kirsty and Matt alone with their baby. She was due for a tea break but she didn't want to risk having it in the staff kitchen and bumping into Xavier so she escaped to the nursery, looking for Sarah. She needed to debrief.

Brighde offered to take over from the other nurse on duty so she could take a tea break which allowed her to talk to Sarah without interruption. The nursery was quiet. It was three o'clock in the morning and most of the babies were with their mothers. Sarah was feeding a premmie baby and there was another who needed changing. Brighde picked her up, changing her nappy before holding her for a while.

She loved the weight of a newborn baby in her arms. Loved the new baby smell. She would love one of her own if things were different.

'Are you going to tell me how it went?' Sarah asked as she settled her charge.

'Fine,' Brighde replied. 'Good, even.' Xavier was a good doctor but Brighde hadn't been able to think straight. She needed a plan. A way of knowing she was going to be able to hold herself together and do her job. She couldn't afford to be distracted.

'And?' Sarah queried. 'You obviously have something on your mind. Spit it out.'

'He asked me out.'

'And you said yes?'

'I don't do second dates. You know that.'

'Technically, it's not a second date. You never really had a first one and a good bonking is not the same thing as a candlelit dinner. And I've never seen you so obsessed.'

'I'm not obsessed,' Brighde objected.

'Fascinated then.'

'Well, there's a lot to be fascinated about,' she admitted.

'There's no harm in going on a date with him. Especially as you can call this a first date.'

'I don't need anyone else in my life. I have you and Nick and now Imogen.'

'Would it be so terrible to have one more?'

'You know I can't afford to let other people close.'

Brighde would love to fall in love but that was a risk she couldn't afford to take. She was worried she wouldn't be able to resist Xavier. She was worried that he'd only have to look at her with those eyes and she'd melt into a pool of desire and do whatever he asked of her. She got all hot and bothered just *thinking* about him.

'Well, say no then. It's as simple as that. You have two choices. Yes or no.'

'It's hard to say no to the best sex of my life.'

'In that case—' Sarah sighed '—maybe you should have another go. Perhaps you're putting him on a pedestal. Perhaps it will be easier to let go if you find out he wasn't so fantastic after all.'

Brighde didn't think that would be the conclusion she'd come to. She couldn't possibly sleep with him again. That would be risking too much. The way her body reacted to him, she knew the fire would burn just as brightly the next time. The heat would be just as intense and she couldn't afford to let her guard down. Something about Xavier made her feel that it would be all too easy to lose control. There was something insanely attractive about him. She *had* to resist. It would be too dangerous not to.

'I can't,' she said. Not sure who she was trying to convince.

She had thought that perhaps more sex was the way to put him out of her mind but she didn't think that more sex with Xavier was the answer.

But it was an answer.

CHAPTER FOUR

BRIGHDE HAD MANAGED to avoid Xavier for the best part of a week but her luck ran out on Wednesday night, when she last expected to see him. She knew he had Wednesday afternoons off—she'd checked—so she was surprised to quite literally bump into him in the hospital corridor.

Just the sight of him set her heart racing. Her palms were sweaty and her throat dry throat as she struggled to form a coherent sentence. 'I thought it was your afternoon off.'

'There was a baby with other ideas,' he told her. 'But I'm finished now. Safely delivered. Are you on your way home too?' he asked and she saw him glance at her bag that was slung over her shoulder.

Brighde nodded.

'Can I walk you to your car?'

'I'm catching a bus.'

'At this time of night?'

'I do it all the time. I only have to get to North Carlton.'

'Let me give you a lift,' he offered as they headed out of the hospital. 'My car is in the doctors' car park.'

That was closer than the bus. Brighde didn't think it would count if she let him drop her home. She didn't have to ask him in. And she would be home much faster. She could think of a dozen good reasons to accept his offer. So she did. 'Thanks, that would be great.'

She sank gratefully into the leather seat. The car smelt new but in the close confines she could also smell Xavier. She remembered his scent. Part shampoo with traces of pear and honey and part man.

Her stomach growled as he turned the car into Lygon Street. 'Do you want to grab something to eat? Not dinner,' he clarified with a quick glance at her, 'just a snack.' She could see him smiling. In profile the corner of his delicious mouth turned up; he obviously thought he was going to win this round.

But she *was* starving. Surely there was no harm in grabbing a quick bite to eat in a public place? No risk.

'Okay.'

'Really?'

She nodded, pleased that she had surprised him. 'I'm starving,' she admitted, just in case he thought it was his company she couldn't resist.

'Italian?' he asked as he pulled to the kerb.

It was close to midnight and there weren't a lot of restaurants still open but Italian sounded good. They ordered bowls of pasta accompanied by a glass of wine. The pasta smelt fantastic but the wine left a metallic taste in Brighde's mouth. She pushed it to one side and concentrated on her pasta.

They chatted about work and which football teams they supported. Nice, neutral, typically Melbourne conversation and Brighde wondered if this was how normal people felt. Was this what it felt like when you actually wanted to get to know someone? Was this what a proper date felt like? Was this how people behaved when they hoped it might lead to something more? She'd never been out with anyone she'd slept with before. Things always ended after that. She'd never let herself have a second date.

She waited until Xavier was halfway through his dish before asking, 'So is now the time you tell me why you came back to Australia?'

'Was that part of the deal?'

Brighde nodded. 'I think it was.'

'There were lots of reasons. I'd been away for four years and my parents aren't getting any younger. I wanted to spend some time with them.'

'Are you close to your family?'

'I am but it's kind of hard not to be. I'm the middle of five siblings, two older sisters, two younger sisters. It's impossible not to get caught up in all the craziness.'

'Wow! Five!'

'And eight nieces and nephews.'

Hearing that made Brighde wistful. Her family had been torn apart, and then depleted, due to disease. Her father had left when she was only nine. Unable to cope with her mother's illness, he had abandoned his family and Brighde had never come to terms with that. How could someone walk out on the people that supposedly meant the world to them? People they loved? She would never put her faith in love. Happily ever after endings were for other people. Other families.

Her mum had succumbed to the disease and for the past five years it had just been Brighde and her brother. That was all that remained of the Campbells now and she wouldn't be adding to the family tree, although she was looking forward to Nick and Imogen having a family. It was nice to think their family would still grow even if it wasn't going to be her doing.

'Do you want kids?' she asked.

'Definitely.'

He sounded so certain and Brighde knew then that she had to cross him off her list. Her silly fantasies about what might be had to stop. She should get up and walk out right now. There was absolutely no point in getting to know him—their paths were headed in completely different directions—but she couldn't make herself leave. Not yet. She could share a meal with him tonight and tomorrow she'd start again.

'What about you?' Now it was Xavier's turn to ask the questions.

'I'm in no hurry,' she said, using her usual excuse. 'I get my fill at work.' She couldn't answer honestly. She couldn't bring herself to tell him 'no'. She knew that would just open her up to a whole lot of questions that she didn't want to answer.

The waitress cleared their plates and Xavier ordered dessert. One serve of tiramisu with two spoons. Brighde didn't think she could fit another thing in but when it arrived it looked so good she couldn't resist. She wondered what was happening to her willpower. She'd have to watch herself around Xavier.

'So, how come you haven't found the mother

of your children yet?' She steered the conversation back to him. 'You didn't fall in love in Scotland?'

A dark expression flashed across his face. It could have been sorrow or pain but it was gone so quickly she wondered if she'd imagined it and she certainly didn't have time to interpret it. Maybe he was just tired or didn't like being questioned. Maybe he really wasn't the talkative type. They certainly hadn't talked much on first meeting.

'No. Scottish girls are not my type.'

'So you've come home to settle down?'

'No. It was always my plan to come back at some stage. Now seemed like a good time but my focus at the moment is work. I'm in no hurry to start a family. I'm going to focus on my work. Build up my practice, get established back here. I don't have time for other distractions.'

Brighde relaxed. It didn't sound as if he was looking for anything more than she could offer at the moment. Maybe they could share one more night without any expectations.

'None?' she teased.

'Well, maybe a couple of distractions would be okay.' The corners of his mouth lifted into a smile. His gorgeous lips were closed; it was only a half-smile but she knew exactly what he was thinking. She could see it in his eyes. They were dark and languid. Just begging her to take him to bed.

Was she prepared to break her own rule? Just this once?

She knew it would be dangerous but she was sorely tempted.

He stood and pulled some cash from his wallet and tucked it under his wineglass before holding her chair for her. He held out his hand to help her up and kept hold of her hand as they left the restaurant. It felt nice, almost as if they were on a real date.

Her house was only a couple of blocks away. They didn't talk as he drove her home. Brighde couldn't think of anything sensible to say. All she could think of was what she should do when they got home. She knew if she invited him in he would accept. It was a big risk but one worth taking. She wanted one more chance. She wanted one more opportunity to commit everything about him to memory.

'It's that house there,' she told him as they drove past a single level terrace house. 'You can drop me out the front if you like,' she offered. Maybe that was one way to resist temptation. The only way.

But Xavier was going to be a complete gentleman. 'No, it's late and it's dark. I'll just find a gap and walk you to your door.'

Sarah was working a night shift and the house was in darkness but Brighde knew the porch light would come on as soon as she opened the front gate.

Xavier parked the car several houses away—parking spaces were hard to find—and followed her through the gate and up the front path. The outside light clicked on and Brighde slid her key into the front door and turned to thank him for the lift.

He was standing centimetres from her. His

eyes were dark and serious and she knew exactly what he was thinking.

'Don't look at me like that,' she said.

'Like what?' He grinned and his eyes lightened. 'Like I want to peel off all your clothes and make love to you again?'

Brighde nodded. She was lost for words. That was exactly the look in his come-to-bed eyes.

She couldn't think when he was looking at her like that.

'But that's exactly what I want to do,' he said. 'Are you going to invite me in?'

Brighde's eyes were fastened on his mouth, reading his words as they fell from his lips.

She started to speak, intending to be strong, intending to tell him 'no', but Xavier bent his head and claimed her lips with his, silencing her words and dissolving all her objections.

She lifted her hands, intending to put them on his chest, intending to push him away, but instead she found her arms winding around his neck, holding him closer.

She thought about telling him to stop but as

his tongue parted her lips her final resistance crumbled.

She wanted this. She wanted one more night.

Was that really so bad?

His hands were under her buttocks and he scooped her up. She wrapped her legs around his hips as he pushed the unlocked door open with his foot and carried her inside.

'First door on the left,' she managed to tell him.

He didn't let her go until they were in her room. He lowered her to the bed but by now her fingers were tearing at the buttons on his shirt. She pulled his shirt from his trousers before unbuckling his belt and unzipping him. Now that she'd made her decision she wasn't about to change her mind.

Xavier pushed his trousers from his hips, exploding from the confines of his clothing, as he stepped out of his shoes.

The only light in the room came through the curtains from the porch but that was enough to illuminate him in all his glory.

He bent over and slid his hands under her skirt. His fingers were warm and firm as he slipped them beneath the elastic of her underwear and pulled them off. Next his fingers slid the zips down on her boots and he removed them and tossed them to one side as she reached for him.

Her fingers wrapped around his erection. His shaft was thick and hard and he moaned and moved closer.

Brighde was on the edge of her bed, still almost fully clothed but she didn't care. There was no time to get undressed; she was in too much of a hurry.

Xavier knelt on the floor and parted her legs. His fingers slid inside her. She was warm and wet and ready.

She inhaled and let her knees fall further apart. Then his fingers were gone and she was about to beg him not to stop when she saw he was reaching for his trousers. He pulled his wallet out, searching for protection. He rolled the sheath on and she lifted her hips and wrapped her legs behind him as he thrust into her, filling her.

His arms were under her shoulders, controlling her movements, holding them together. Brighde threw her head back but fought to keep her eyes open as waves of pleasure rolled through her. She wanted to watch him. His eyes were fixed on her, taking it all in as he took her.

They were keeping time to the same orchestra, their bodies perfectly in tune. Xavier rolled his thumb over her swollen sweet spot and Brighde thought she was going to burst into a thousand tiny pieces.

'Oh, God, Xavier.'

She heard him hold his breath, felt him start to come and she cried out as he knelt between her thighs and brought them both to a climax.

Xavier collapsed on the bed beside her and wrapped her in his arms.

'Can you stay?' she asked, hating the fact that she was asking but she really didn't want him to leave. She wanted him to stay the night. She wanted to get completely naked and make love again, one final time. She wasn't ready for it to end just yet.

He nodded and kissed her.

She sat up and unzipped her skirt, sliding it from her body. She lifted her arms and Xavier pulled her shirt over her head. He undid her bra with one flick of his fingers and bent his head to her breast. Brighde lay back as Xavier's tongue circled her nipple. Their initial frenzied desire had been sated; she knew that she would have a chance to take it slow this time, to savour every second and commit it all to memory.

She'd broken all her rules for him in just one night. She never spent a second night with a man. She never invited them to her house and she definitely had never slept with someone she worked with. But she was finding him difficult to resist. She'd have to come up with a new plan but that could wait until tomorrow. For tonight she was staying right where she was. She fell asleep in his arms, her head on his chest, lulled to sleep by the rise and fall of his chest and the sound of his breaths.

* * *

'Good morning.'

Brighde woke to the sound of his voice. He brushed a strand of hair from her cheek as he leant down to kiss her. He was already out of bed and dressed. 'I need to get home and shower for work,' he said. 'What are your plans for the day?'

Brighde took a moment to remember what day it was. 'I'm having brunch with my brother and his fiancée and then I'm on another afternoon shift.'

'Shall I come and pick you up after work? I could give you a lift home again.'

It was clear he wanted to continue on from last night. Brighde liked the sound of that. She was flattered but she knew she shouldn't accept. She couldn't start something with Xavier. They shouldn't have even had last night.

'I'd like that,' she said, meaning to add *'but I can't'* but the words never made it out.

Xavier grinned and kissed her again. 'I'll see you later then,' he said.

She rolled over in bed and watched him leave. She wondered what it would be like to be like normal people and make real plans for the day or the week or next weekend. She knew she needed to be careful; Xavier was testing the limits of her willpower. She knew she would never make plans for the rest of her life but waking up with someone and knowing she would see him again felt nice.

Was this how it had started for Nick and Imogen? Had Nick's plans crumbled in the face of his feelings for Immy? She'd love to ask him but she didn't want that to lead to questions about what was going on in her life.

Nick and Imogen were waiting for her at the café.

'Are you feeling okay?' Imogen asked her as she gave her a hug.

Brighde knew she looked pale and washed out. Hardly the glow of someone who'd spent a passionate night in bed with the sexiest man alive. She had dark circles under her eyes and really needed to spend more than two minutes on her make-up but she'd run out of time and hadn't wanted to keep Nick and Immy waiting.

'I didn't get a lot of sleep last night.' She knew they'd assume it was because of work and she was happy to let them think that. She wasn't prepared to talk about Xavier. Talking about a man would be completely out of character for her and would only invite questions she wasn't prepared to even think about, let alone answer.

'We've got some good news,' Nick told her as the waitress took their order. This was a regular meeting spot for them and Brighde always ordered the same breakfast. Eggs Benedict with Hollandaise sauce.

'You've picked a date for the wedding?' Brighde guessed.

'No, that's next on our to-do list.' Nick held Imogen's hand. A gesture that looked so tender and sweet that Brighde felt a pang of longing. 'We're having a baby.'

'It's a bit sooner than we planned but we're really excited,' Imogen said.

'A baby! Wow.' Brighde sat back in her seat as she digested the news. 'I'm going to be an auntie.'

She smiled. It was good news. Happy news. Nick's negative test results meant that he and Imogen could start a family without any concerns about passing on the mutated gene. Brighde would love to have a family of her own and while she knew that was a possibility with the assistance of genetic testing she wasn't going to risk putting her own children through what she and Nick had gone through with their mother. Watching their mother deteriorate and eventually die at a young age had been horrific and it was something Brighde had no intention of repeating. But Nick and Imogen didn't need to worry about that. That worry was Brighde's alone now.

Brighde didn't want to think about how alike she and her mother were. Nick and Brighde had the same colouring—they were both blonde and with the same blue-grey eyes—but Nick was tall and lean and his face was longer than hers, not as square, although he still had a very defined jawline. They were similar enough that people recognised them as siblings but Brighde was the spitting image of her mother while Nick had more of their father in him. Because of the similarities in appearance between her and her mother she had always assumed they'd be alike in other ways too. Right down to the faulty DNA.

But Brighde didn't want to think about her mother today. It always made her sad and today she wanted to be happy for Nick. 'Congratulations. I'm really happy for you.' She stood up to hug them both again, determined not to let her dark thoughts ruin their excitement.

'We thought it might take longer to happen, so as soon as we got my test results we started trying.'

'How many weeks are you?' she asked Imogen.

'Only eight, but we couldn't wait to tell someone. We knew you'd understand.'

She did understand the excitement and she

was happy for them but it didn't stop her from wishing things were different for her. She'd have to be content with being an auntie—that was almost as good as having a family of her own.

'We'll have to move the wedding forward now,' Nick was saying. 'I'd like to be married before the baby comes. Make an honest woman of you.'

He was looking at his fiancée with such adoration that it made Brighde's heart ache.

'That shouldn't be hard,' Imogen replied. 'There's only a few people we really want to be there with us. You,' she said, looking at Brighde, 'my parents and my sister.'

'What about Dad?' Brighde asked. She knew that Nick had some contact with their father. She had severed all ties with him when he'd walked out on them and their mother but, as an adult, Nick had reconnected with him and they caught up occasionally.

'That's up to you,' he said. 'If having him there would make you uncomfortable then we won't invite him. It's more important to me—to us—' he smiled and picked up Imogen's hand '—that you'll be there. We'd like you to be our witness.'

Brighde smiled. 'I'd be honoured.'

'Thank you,' Imogen said as she stood up. 'I'll be back in a minute.'

'I really am happy for you, Nick. The two of you are going to have a beautiful life.'

'You might be able to have the same. Have you thought any more about getting tested?'

Brighde shook her head. 'Nothing has changed for me. I didn't want to get tested before and I definitely don't want to get tested now. I don't want to know and part of me feels even more certain that it would only be bad news. I'm okay as I am.' She was more convinced than ever that she had inherited her mother's DNA and she really didn't want to know that she'd be going to an early grave. It was far better just to avoid going down the path of marriage and babies.

Imogen returned to the table carrying two glasses of champagne. 'I can't have any but I thought we could toast the baby,' she said as she handed Nick and Brighde each a glass.

'To your family,' Brighde said as she raised her glass. She put it to her lips to take a sip but the yeasty smell turned her stomach. She forced down a sip so she didn't appear rude and then put her glass on the table.

'I might just wait until I've had something to eat,' she said. Drinking on an empty stomach and on top of a limited amount of sleep seemed like a recipe for disaster.

'You sound like how I feel in the morning,' Imogen said. 'I'll be pleased when my morning sickness stops.'

'Well, I don't envy you that.'

Brighde didn't finish her champagne and even her breakfast sat heavily in her stomach as she walked home. She was feeling a little queasy. Perhaps she was coming down with a cold. She'd felt a bit flat for the past few mornings, she realised, but once she'd got to work and was busy she'd been okay.

Her symptoms were mimicking Imogen's

morning sickness but Brighde knew she was only thinking that way because of all the baby talk at brunch.

She couldn't be pregnant.

But her last period had been exceptionally light.

Surely that didn't mean anything?

The idea of it made her feel queasy and her legs were shaky. She stopped walking and rested her hand on a street bench as she waited for the queasiness to pass.

She looked up and saw she was outside a pharmacy.

There was only one way to make sure.

She went inside and bought a pregnancy test kit.

She took it home and went straight to the bathroom.

CHAPTER FIVE

'WHAT ARE YOU doing in here?'

The bathroom door opened and Sarah stepped in. Her hair was dishevelled and Brighde realised she'd just woken up after working a night shift.

Brighde hadn't realised how long she'd been sitting in the bathroom. She hadn't been able to make herself move after taking the test. Waves of nausea had swamped her and she'd vomited a couple of times. But she refused to think the vomiting was symptomatic; she was sure it was stress-related.

'Are you sick?' Sarah asked.

'Not exactly,' Brighde said as she pointed to the stick sitting on the side of the bath.

'Oh, my God.' Sarah was looking at her in shock. 'You're *pregnant*?'

Brighde nodded.

'How the hell did that happen?'

'I don't know.' She was on the Pill and she took it religiously and also practised safe sex. She'd always been afraid that one mistake would mean something like this might happen.

'Didn't you use a condom?'

'I think so.' She honestly couldn't remember. It was weeks ago. It would have been very unlike her to be so careless but she really couldn't recall. How could she not remember? How could she be so reckless? But what did it matter now? The *how* was irrelevant. She was pregnant and what mattered now was doing something about it and there was only one option in her mind.

'Are you going to tell Xavier?'

She shook her head. 'No. He doesn't need to know. I'm not going to keep it,' she said before bursting into tears. Termination had always been her fallback position and she knew that was her only option, but she wished just for a moment that things could be different.

Sarah hugged her. 'My God, you're freezing.'

Brighde had been sitting in the bathroom for so long the cold had seeped into her bones. She was shaking now with shock and cold.

'You need to go to bed,' Sarah told her. 'There's nothing we can do about this right now. I'll bring you a cup of tea and then I'll call the hospital and cancel your shift.'

'Xavier!' Surprise was written all over Sarah's face when she opened the front door, answering his knock. 'What are you doing here?'

'I heard Brighde was sick,' he said. 'I brought her some of my mum's chicken soup.' He held up the container as evidence of his good intentions.

'That's really sweet but I don't think that's going to help.'

'What's wrong with her?' he asked. She'd been fine that morning so when he'd heard that she'd called in sick he'd figured it couldn't be much more than a gastro bug or something similar.

'She's in bed—do you want to see her?' Sarah

asked as she took the soup and stepped back, letting him into the hall.

He followed Sarah to the back of the house, walking past Brighde's room. 'I'll just wash my hands,' he said. He didn't want to expose Brighde to any more germs but as he washed his hands he realised Sarah hadn't answered his question. He dried his hands and returned the towel to the hook that hung over the rubbish bin. A box for a pregnancy test kit poked up out of the bin and caught his eye. He reached for the bin and then hesitated. Was this any of his business?

He dropped his hand to his side, resisting the urge to pick up the kit.

But his heart was beating furiously in his chest and his mouth had gone dry. He needed to see the kit. He needed to see the result.

His hand shook as he picked up the empty box and exposed the little stick that lay in the bin underneath.

He could see two pink lines in the window.

Someone in this house was pregnant.

He lifted the stick from the bin and carried it out of the bathroom.

Sarah was in the kitchen, boiling the kettle. She turned when she heard him enter. 'Would you like…?' The question died on her lips when she saw what he was holding.

'Is this yours?' he asked.

Her eyes were wide with fright but she shook her head and he had his answer.

His heart was hammering in his chest. He could feel the blood pumping in his neck, flooding his carotid artery. Sarah was biting her lip. Was she wondering what he was going to do next?

He felt dazed, sucker-punched, but he knew he had to talk to Brighde. He had to find out what was going on.

He left the kitchen, still holding the test stick, and knocked on Brighde's door. He didn't wait for permission to enter. He was going in, no matter what she said. They had things to discuss.

'Brighde?' he said as he pushed the door open.

Her bedside lamp was on, bathing the room in a soft yellow light. Her blonde hair was tousled and thick. Her face pale and tearstained.

He sat on the edge of her bed and put the stick on her bedside table. He saw her eyes dart to the stick, widen and then look back at him.

'Where did you—?'

'I found it in the bathroom,' he said, cutting her off. 'You're pregnant?'

Her eyes were enormous, grey and frightened, as she nodded.

'Is it mine?'

Brighde wanted to be offended that he'd asked her that but she knew it was a legitimate question.

'Yes. There hasn't been anyone since you and I...' She drifted off, letting him fill in the blanks. Despite the impression he might have of her, she didn't jump in and out of men's beds on a regular basis. Once or twice a year for one night didn't make her promiscuous. Not in her opinion anyway, but she wasn't about to share the finer details of her love life with him.

She sat up in bed. This wasn't the place she'd envisaged having this conversation. If she was going to be brutally honest, she hadn't planned on having this conversation at all. She had thought the best thing to do was not to say anything to him and just deal with it as she thought best. She knew he would want to keep the baby and that was not her plan. The less said the better, in her opinion. But it looked as if that option had been taken away from her.

'Wow.'

He said nothing more for a moment. He just sat and stared into the distance.

Brighde waited. She had no idea what to say so thought it best to stay silent.

'This is huge,' he said eventually. 'We have to work out what we're going to do.'

'There's nothing to work out,' she told him. 'I know what I'm going to do and don't worry, I won't put any pressure on you. I don't intend to keep it.'

'What?'

Xavier sat back, reacting as if she'd slapped

him, his gorgeous face showing his complete shock. But he shouldn't be so surprised. She'd told him she wasn't ready to have children of her own. Ironic that she'd only mentioned it last night.

'I know you said that you get your fill of babies at work,' he said, clearly remembering the conversation, 'but surely this has changed things?'

She shook her head. 'No, it hasn't.'

'I understand this is unexpected, a shock even, and it may be sooner than you would have planned but you're *pregnant*. That *must* change things?'

'No.'

'Surely you haven't come to that decision so quickly? Surely you'll consider your options?'

'To be honest, I didn't decide overnight not to go ahead with the pregnancy. I decided that a long time ago. I never intended to have children.'

'Never? You must have planned to have children of your own at some point.'

'No.'

'We're not even going to discuss this?'

'There's nothing to discuss. I'm not keeping it.' Brighde took a deep breath. 'I know you want kids but I didn't think you wanted them right now. You told me you wanted to concentrate on your work. I imagine your plan of fatherhood is vastly different to this situation too. I can't imagine you thought you'd have a baby with someone you barely know. You didn't sign up for this and I definitely didn't.'

She was counting on the fact that he wasn't any more prepared to become a parent than she was.

'I realise it's not ideal,' he said, 'and maybe I'm not the man you had in mind to be the father of your children, but can't we discuss this?'

'This isn't about you and what sort of parent you'd be. I've never even *thought* about the type of man I'd look for as a father to my kids. It was a moot point, considering I decided a long time ago that I wasn't ever having children.'

'But that's crazy! That must have been a hypothetical discussion you had with yourself? Surely this situation changes things?'

Brighde shook her head. 'No, it doesn't.'

'How can you say that? I think you should take some time, we both should, and let this sink in.'

'I'm not going to change my mind.'

'How do you know?'

'It's complicated,' she said. Although that was a lie. It wasn't complicated, in her opinion.

'I think you owe me an explanation.'

Brighde sighed. 'I know I do.' It was only fair. To him. Not to her. None of this was fair to her. She'd always tried to ensure she would *never* find herself in this position. Nothing about this was fair. And there was no easy way to start this conversation. She took a deep breath. 'Have you ever had a patient who suffers from Huntington's Disease?'

'Huntington's Chorea?'

She nodded.

'Not that I can recall.'

'Do you remember anything about the disease from your training?'

He frowned. 'A little. It's an inherited condition, right? That causes degeneration in the brain and affects movement. Which is where the term "chorea" comes from.'

'It's a genetic mutation that ultimately kills the nerve cells in the brain. It affects mood, memory and movement and results in premature death. There is no cure.' She hesitated very briefly, dreading the idea that she had to have this conversation but knowing she couldn't avoid it. 'As you said, it's an inherited condition. It runs in families and my mother had it.'

'Had?'

Brighde nodded. 'She died five years ago. She was forty-nine. The mutation is a dominant one. There's a one in two chance of children inheriting the fault and therefore developing the disease. I have one brother; he doesn't have the mutation.'

His face went pale under the dark stubble that lined his jaw. 'Are you telling me you do?'

'There's a strong possibility.'

'Don't you know? You said there's no cure but surely there's a test for it?'

'There is but I've never been tested.'

'So there's a good chance you don't have it?' Xavier's shoulders relaxed as he let out a breath she hadn't noticed him holding.

'I wouldn't say a good chance. My brother tested negative. If there's a fifty-fifty chance of inheriting the gene and he didn't get it, I reckon the odds are not in my favour.'

'But why haven't you been tested to make sure?'

'I don't want to know.'

'How does that work?' He was frowning now. 'How can you not want to know?'

Brighde, like many other people whose lives had been affected by Huntington's, had her reasons and, to her, they sounded logical, sensible and reasonable. But she had to try to explain it in a way that would make Xavier understand. She knew that was vitally important.

'Imagine if you were told today that you

were going to be hit by a bus and killed in five years' time. Would you want to know? Would it change the way you live your life?'

'I think it probably would.'

'What if you were told you were going to be hit by a bus at the age of forty and that you'd survive but you wouldn't be able to walk or talk any more? That, more than likely, you'd lose your memories and you wouldn't be able to communicate. Would you want to know that your future looked like that?'

'That doesn't sound appealing.'

'Trust me, it's not. Nick and I watched our mother suffer that exact fate and it's horrible. Knowing your life is heading in that direction might make you determined to pack as much into the days you have left, but what about when your fortieth birthday gets closer? What about when it's a month, a week, a day away—how do you think you'll feel then, knowing what is about to happen? How would your family cope with that scenario? I don't want to know if my life is going to end prematurely. I watched my mother die and I don't want to know if that is my future too. I'm happier not knowing. That's why I haven't been tested.'

'I think I understand but I don't see how this means you want to terminate a pregnancy. You don't know if you have the faulty gene and you don't know if our child does either. We're talking in hypotheticals.'

'There's every chance I have the mutation. Nick and I nursed our mother until we couldn't manage. We had to put her into care and then we watched her deteriorate a little more every day until she died. I'm not going to put anyone I love through that and especially not my own child.'

'But don't you see, you don't know for certain what you're faced with?'

'But what if *I've* passed on the gene? How do you think you would feel watching your child die before you? I can only think of one thing worse than watching my mother die and that is watching my own child suffer and die. I can't do it.'

'But you might not have to. You could get tested and then make a decision.'

Xavier picked up her hand and held it. It was a surprisingly comforting gesture but it didn't change anything.

'You're not listening to me,' she said as she pulled her hand from his grasp. She couldn't think when he was touching her. 'I really don't want to know what my future holds. I don't think Nick and I could both be that lucky and I don't want to live with the knowledge of a premature death and what that looks like. I don't want to pass on this gene. I don't want to be pregnant.'

She was scared. She was terrified. She couldn't do this.

'I think we're probably both in a bit of shock. There's a lot to think about but we don't need to make decisions tonight. We have time. It's what…ten weeks since the conference?'

'Nine and a half.' Which made her eleven and a half weeks pregnant.

'Please. Don't make any hasty decisions. Can

we both take some time to think about what this means and talk about it some more?'

He could talk about it all he liked but she wasn't going to change her mind. But she nodded anyway. It was easier to give in for now. It didn't mean she had to change her mind and she was going to go crazy if she had to talk about it any more tonight.

'Do you want company?' he asked.

'No.' She shook her head. 'I want to be alone.' Seeing Xavier would just remind her of the situation she was in. If he wasn't there she could pretend it was all a nightmare.

Xavier's head was spinning when he left Brighde.

She was pregnant!

He was going to be a father.

He wanted kids, had always wanted them, and he made no secret of the fact to those nearest to him. He'd grown up in a close family, doted on by his sisters and, in turn, he doted on his nieces and nephews but he wanted children of his own. He'd actually thought he'd be a father already—he'd certainly thought he was on the way with his ex until she had ripped his dreams from him. But that hadn't deterred him. To acquaintances he said he was concentrating on his career but that was what people expected a man to say. He'd always intended to have children, a family of his own, and he knew he could do both. Granted, this current situation wasn't exactly what he had in mind but that didn't mean he was prepared to give up his dream. Not again.

He wanted to be a father. He was *going* to be a father, only that wasn't Brighde's plan.

He could understand her anxiety but to him things were black and white. He dealt in facts and figures, not in suppositions. He knew emotions could influence decisions—he saw that every day in his job—but he didn't believe that emotion should be the deciding factor, not without the facts. Brighde was making decisions based on assumptions. He wasn't discounting her experiences but she wasn't being reasonable. In his experience, you gathered the facts and then you dealt with them. You didn't worry about things that hadn't happened yet.

He could acknowledge her fear but he wasn't going to give in to it. She *had* to get tested. He couldn't let her make such a monumental decision without gathering all the facts. Ultimately, he might not stand in her way but that was a discussion for another day. A day when they had some facts to deal with.

He started his car and pulled into the traffic.

He didn't want to go. He didn't want to leave her alone. She'd said she needed space and he would respect that, but it was hard to leave.

He wanted to comfort her but he realised he probably also needed some time to clear his head. They obviously had differing opinions on this situation and if he was going to convince her to see his point of view he needed time to work out a strategy. There was a lot of information to take in, a lot to think about.

She was scared; he got that. He wanted to erase her fears but he needed information.

She was talking about terminating the pregnancy. He wanted her to keep the baby and he needed to work out how he was going to achieve that.

He needed a plan.

Brighde had three days off work and she managed to avoid any further discussion. She ignored Xavier's phone calls and only replied to his text messages very briefly, telling him she wasn't ready to talk yet. But after three days she was going stir crazy in the house, alone with her thoughts.

She pounced on Sarah when she walked through the door after her shift. 'How was work?' she asked, desperate for news of the outside world. Of Xavier. Not that she would admit it.

'Quiet. No dramatics today.'

'Who were you working with?'

'Paul Davey,' Sarah replied. She paused slightly before she added, 'You could always call him, you know.'

'Who? Paul? What for?'

'You know I don't mean Paul. Xavier.'

'Have you seen him?'

'Yes.'

'Did he ask about me?'

'No.' Sarah shook her head. 'I'm sorry.'

Was it a good thing or a bad thing that Xavier wasn't asking about her? Brighde didn't know. Part of her wanted him to worry about her. She wanted him to tell her everything would be all right, even though she knew that was unlikely. If he was worried about anything it would be about the baby and what her plans were.

'I think you should call him,' Sarah said. 'You need to talk about this. You can't keep avoiding the topic. It's not going to go away on its own.'

Brighde knew that. She knew she would have to make a move. She couldn't delay the inevitable. She had to make plans but she didn't have to discuss them with Xavier, yet she knew that was the decent thing to do. She was going to have to continue to work with him. She couldn't pretend this hadn't happened and she couldn't terminate the pregnancy without another conversation with him. He was no longer an anonymous one-night stand. He was her colleague and she knew more about him than she wanted to. He seemed like a good person; he deserved some consideration. This wasn't all his fault; she had to take some of the blame, and therefore some of the responsibility. She knew she needed to speak to him but it was a daunting task.

She still intended to terminate the pregnancy. She didn't need Xavier's permission but part of her wanted it. In her mind, when she'd thought about what she'd do if she was ever faced with this decision, there was never a father of the baby that needed her consideration. She'd never envisaged this scenario.

But now there was very much a father in the picture. She couldn't deny that but she still wasn't ready to see him. She didn't want to give him an opportunity to try to talk her out of her decision.

But she knew she couldn't avoid him for ever. She was due back at work tomorrow.

* * *

She had half hoped he wouldn't be on the ward today but she'd barely finished handover when he found her.

'Hi, how are you?' His voice wrapped around her like a comforting hug and made her want to step into his arms. She could use a hug.

'Good,' she lied, as she fought back tears. She was an emotional wreck and she knew she looked like she'd been through the wringer. She was pale, tired and unhappy. Xavier, by comparison, looked gorgeous. His eyes were bright, his hair was shiny, thick and healthy, his skin lightly tanned.

'Brighde, I have four sisters and I work with women all day. I can tell when a woman is lying.'

'Okay. Since you asked, I've been throwing up constantly—' morning sickness had arrived with a vengeance '—I'm exhausted, physically, emotionally and mentally. I've barely slept. The whole thing is a nightmare. Is there anything else you want to know?' She had a slight sense that she was being cruel but she couldn't help it. This situation was partly his fault. Why should he get off scot-free? If he pulled her up for being harsh she could always blame a lack of sleep and an excess of hormones.

'I need to ask you something.' He put his hand on her elbow and steered her towards a quiet spot in the corridor.

'Oh, God, Xavier, not now.' He couldn't possibly want to have the conversation she'd been trying to avoid, here at work? She felt her eyes widen with panic and her heart was racing. Was she going to throw up again? Early shifts were perhaps not the best for her in her state and if he was going to put her under the pump she didn't think she would cope with that *and* morning sickness.

'What do you take me for?' he said and she could hear the offence in his voice. 'It's a work question.'

'Oh. Sorry.' Perhaps she wasn't giving him enough credit. He hadn't really done anything wrong.

Except get her pregnant.

'You're taking over Amelia's patient in labour, correct?'

'Yes.'

'I'm the obstetrician. There's a slight problem and I told Amelia I would discuss it with you.'

'With labour?' Brighde frowned. It was unusual for the doctors to seek out the midwives in order to discuss their patients. Usually any issues were raised during handover.

'Not exactly.'

'Don't you want to work with me?' Maybe that was what this was about. Nothing to do with the patient and everything to do with trust?

'No, it's nothing like that. I have no issue working with you.'

Did he have other issues with her? She supposed it was highly likely but she was happy to avoid that topic as he continued. 'Labour is going well but this delivery isn't totally straightforward and I wanted to talk to you about it in private.' He paused and took a deep breath, giving Brighde the impression that he was steeling himself for something. 'The baby has Down Syndrome.'

'Do the parents know?' Brighde asked before she held her breath, waiting for his answer. She hated those deliveries where the parents were expecting a normal, straightforward delivery of a healthy baby and things didn't quite go to plan.

'They do.'

Brighde breathed out. That was good. No surprises was a good thing.

'And they are looking forward to a normal delivery and to welcoming this child into their family. They want the experience to be joyful and they have specifically requested that the staff are aware of their wishes and that the staff will respect the fact that this baby is loved and wanted. I need to know how you feel about that. Whether you can give them what they want or if you want to swap patients with one of the other midwives?'

'You think I can't do my job?'

'I don't know.' He was watching her carefully.

Perhaps he was worried she was going to lose the plot completely. 'Given our last conversation, I wasn't sure how you would cope with this. I need to know that you can give the parents the support and attention they want and need and deserve.'

'Of course,' she replied. The parents had made their decision and she would respect that. Just because she would choose differently didn't mean she would treat them differently or without respect. 'I am not going to judge people for their decisions, just like I hope I'm not judged for mine.'

Let him think about that!

Brighde managed to hold herself together through the delivery and while she settled the new parents and their baby. The baby was beautiful, ten fingers and ten toes and big blue eyes, and Brighde felt the usual pang of longing. But it wasn't enough to convince her to change her mind about her own pregnancy. If anything, despite what she'd told Xavier, she was more adamant now than ever about termination. This family had chosen to welcome their child into the world but there was a difference. This child had Down Syndrome and would lead a normal life within those parameters. In all likelihood, he would lead a long life and wouldn't experience any dramatic changes in quality of life once into adulthood. In Brighde's opinion, one couldn't compare Down Syndrome to Huntington's Disease but when it came down to it the real issue was with her. Bottom line, she didn't think she was strong enough to go through the trauma of suffering from Huntington's herself or watching her child suffer.

But what if she didn't have the mutation? She knew that was a possibility.

Could she be that lucky?

Was she strong enough to risk finding out?

She let the tears that she'd been holding back flow as she washed her hands in the sluice room, hoping for some privacy. She was super emotional at the moment and every emotion—

happiness, sadness, fear—all seemed to be magnified. Especially fear.

'Are you okay?'

His voice made her jump. Was he going to follow her around, constantly checking on her?

'I don't know. I don't even know why I'm crying.' She rinsed her face as she tried to work out how she was feeling. *What* she was feeling. Confused. Guilty. Sad. In equal parts.

'Why don't you come for a walk with me? Get some fresh air and clear your head. You're on your lunch break now, aren't you?'

Xavier needed to talk to her. He'd done some research and he wanted—needed—to talk about their options. He had some suggestions to make and a walk in the garden next to the hospital might be the perfect place to have a neutral discussion. If they walked and talked Brighde wouldn't need to maintain eye contact and then she might feel less like he was pressuring or interrogating her.

'Yes, but surely you don't have time?' she replied.

'I do,' he said. 'Unless another expectant mum goes into labour, I'm good. I want you to know that I'm here to support you and that starts now.'

He waited until they were out in the autumn sunshine before he began. 'I've been doing some research. I was surprised I'd never come across Huntington's Disease, except in theory, but when I found out there are only sixteen hundred Huntington's sufferers in Australia it made more sense.'

'Only sixteen hundred that we know of,' Brighde said.

'But, with the genetic testing that's available now, in a few more generations there could be none. The disease could be eradicated.' He thought this was incredible.

'If people choose to get tested.'

'That's my point. Why wouldn't you get tested if you've got the option?'

'Would *you* want to know that you're going to die a premature death?' she asked again.

Xavier had thought about this since she'd first

posed the question days ago. 'I think I would. I'd like time to prepare.'

'You can't prepare for something like Huntington's Disease. It's not like getting killed in a plane crash,' she said. 'It's not sudden. It's a horrible, debilitating disease. It takes your life slowly over several years. There's no cure. I don't want to know if that's what my future holds.'

'So instead you want to terminate what could potentially be a perfectly healthy pregnancy?' Xavier knew he needed to stay calm and in control but he was really struggling to follow Brighde's logic.

'I know you want children, Xavier. I know that's in your plans for the future but I'm not the one to give them to you. I'm pregnant but it wasn't planned and I don't have to stay pregnant. It's my prerogative.'

'We can do this together.'

'There is no *together*. There is no *we*. We don't have a relationship. And even if we did, this disease destroys lives. My own father walked out when I was nine. He promised to love my mother through sickness and in health and that didn't last. It wasn't enough to make him stick around when the going got tough. How could I expect you to stay and support me if we start out with nothing substantial between us in the first place? I've made my decision. I'm not having this baby. I've made an appointment to see Julie Stewart to discuss a termination.'

Xavier felt as if she'd punched him. His stomach lurched and he had a pain in his chest. If he didn't know better he'd think he was having a cardiac episode but he knew the pain was caused by Brighde's words. He couldn't comprehend that she could so blithely announce that she was going to deprive him of his child. He'd lost a child once before and he couldn't bear to think of it happening again and he would do anything to ensure it didn't. He needed to have some control this time. He knew that would be difficult but he refused to back down quietly. This was his child and he would do everything in his power to make sure he would meet this one.

'Brighde, please. I'm begging you. Can't we discuss this some more?'

She shook her head. 'You're an obstetrician. Surely you've had patients who have had terminations arranged by you? There must be some instances where you agree that it's the right thing to do?'

'Yes,' he admitted. On a couple of occasions where it had been best for the baby or for the mother's health, physically or emotionally, he'd been involved but that was different.

'So what's the difference now?'

'Now it's *my* child we're talking about.' It couldn't be *more* different, in his opinion. But he knew Brighde could do as she pleased. 'But I guess it doesn't matter what I think or what I want. You hold all the cards.'

A termination wasn't necessarily what Brighde wanted either. She would love to be a mother but this was what was best. She didn't need, or even want, Xavier's permission but she did want him to understand her decision. And, hopefully, support it. She didn't want him to think she was being selfish or unemotional. She wanted him to like her. She thought he was fabulous and she wanted him to think the same of her. But she knew that was unlikely, especially given these circumstances, and she wasn't willing to trade her decision for his approval.

Xavier stopped walking and turned to her as he said, 'I know I don't legally have any say in this decision, I understand that, but there's something I'd like to tell you.'

'What is it?' she asked, even as she wondered if she should warn him that there was nothing he could say or do that would convince her to change her mind. She should warn him he was wasting his breath but he looked so desperate to be heard that she couldn't refuse to listen.

He sat on a park bench and Brighde sat with him.

'I wasn't totally upfront with you,' he told her. 'Remember you asked me if I'd fallen in love in Scotland?'

Brighde nodded. 'You said Scottish girls weren't your type.'

'I did. Which wasn't quite true. Three months before I came back home I broke up with my girlfriend.'

'Oh.' Brighde thought about that for a moment, wondering what that had to do with their situation.

'We'd been together for two and a half years.'

Again, Brighde wondered what relevance that had. Then she remembered the expression on his face when she'd asked about his girlfriends. That look she hadn't been able to decipher. Sorrow or pain. Maybe it had been both. 'Were you in love with her?'

'At the time I thought so. And I thought she loved me.'

'You couldn't work things out?'

'No. Things got complicated.'

'What happened?' Surely things couldn't have been more complicated than the circumstances he found himself in now?

'She was pregnant.'

He'd been in this situation before? And last time he'd been in a relationship and things still hadn't worked out, yet he seemed to think they would be able to muddle their way through this. As if things weren't difficult enough.

Was. He'd said was. Something must have happened. Something must have gone wrong because she knew Xavier didn't have children. 'Did she lose the baby?' she asked. That might explain Xavier's expression, might explain the pain and sorrow she'd seen in his eyes, but it didn't necessarily explain the break-up.

'No. We hadn't planned it, hadn't even talked about it really, but I was over the moon. Until she told me that she'd been having an affair. She told me it had started because I spent too much time working. I was doing my speciality training so I figured that it went without saying that I would be doing ridiculous hours, but she figured that seeing I was studying OB/GYN my hours were always going to be ridiculous and she felt she was never going to be my first priority. And then she told me there was a chance the baby wasn't mine.'

No wonder he'd asked if Brighde's baby was his when he'd discovered the positive pregnancy test.

'Anyway, it turned out she was right: the baby wasn't mine.'

'She's had it?'

He nodded.

'And you're sure it's not yours? You're not going back to Scotland to check? To have tests?'

'No. We did the tests while she was pregnant. We did a prenatal paternity test at fourteen weeks. You know the one, a blood sample from her and mouth swabs from the possible fathers. I was excluded as a potential father based on the DNA testing. The baby wasn't mine. And that's when I decided to come home. I needed to come home. I needed a break, to take some time out. Once I got here I realised how much I'd missed Australia and I decided to stay.'

'Are you asking me to have the same test? Is

that why you're telling me this?' Was that why he'd told her this story?

'No. You've told me the baby is mine and I believe you. You didn't have to tell me that. You're probably regretting the fact that you did, given what your plans are, but it seems to me that you're making some big decisions, huge decisions, without all the facts. And these decisions affect me too. And our baby. Won't you at least get the baby tested? Then we'll know what we're dealing with.'

'But that's just it,' she replied. 'I don't *want* to know what we're dealing with. I made the decision long ago *not* to get tested and if I test the baby and the result comes back positive then I will know my fate too. I'm not ready for this.'

Xavier was nodding but he wasn't finished. 'Can I ask you one favour then?'

'What is it?'

'Before you make any further plans would you please have an ultrasound? I'd like a chance to at least see my baby.'

CHAPTER SIX

BRIGHDE LAY ON the exam table and pulled the shirt of her scrubs up and eased the waistband of her pants down, exposing her midriff.

She was a lot quieter than he was used to. She wasn't even giving him any grief and she definitely wasn't making eye contact. He expected she'd agreed to the ultrasound out of a sense of obligation but he didn't care. He was desperate for a glimpse of his baby. He was amazed at how important this was to him. He'd made no secret of the fact that he wanted to be a father, that it was in his plans for the future, but he'd anticipated that, like a lot of other fathers he'd spoken to, the sense of responsibility and love for his offspring wouldn't eventuate until he held his child in his arms. But he already felt an overwhelming sense of responsibility and an urge to protect his unborn child. And that was his second reason for asking Brighde to let him do an ultrasound. He hoped that once she saw the image of her baby—*their* baby—on the screen, she might be more willing to discuss alternatives.

This baby was a gift he hadn't expected and one he would do everything in his power to keep. Despite what had transpired with his ex, or maybe because of it, his dreams of fatherhood were strong. He would have to wait and see how he and Brighde would get through this together but he was determined that they would. Their relationship might not be a traditional one but he wasn't going to let go of his dream. He wasn't going to give up his child without a fight and he was pinning all his hopes and dreams on this scan.

But the procedure wasn't going quite as he'd anticipated. Brighde had given him clear instructions as to how this was going to work. She had agreed to an ultrasound but only an abdominal one. She'd said no to a pelvic one, claiming that seemed far too personal, which was ridiculous considering they'd had sex, but she'd been adamant—he could do the ultrasound abdominally or not at all. But that was okay and it was definitely better than nothing. She was twelve weeks pregnant; an abdominal ultrasound should give him a clear picture.

Her face was stony, expressionless, set, as if she was deliberately blocking all thoughts on what was about to happen. She'd told him she didn't want to look at the monitor. She didn't want to see the baby.

He knew she'd prefer not to be pregnant and he assumed that she didn't want to see the image because that would make it real. He wished she would change her mind but he wasn't about to argue with her now. He was grateful that she'd agreed to the ultrasound at all and he wasn't going to jeopardise this opportunity. She might not want to see their baby but he sure as hell did.

Had she suspected that his motivations for the ultrasound were not completely altruistic? He should have thought about the chance that she would refuse to look at the images. She was a midwife; she'd seen plenty of scans before. She would know what to expect and she would prepare for it. This was obviously her way of preparing—by denying it all. It seemed to be her way of coping.

But this pregnancy was really happening and he just wanted time to convince her not to end it prematurely. He was counting on this ultrasound, but she was playing tough.

Her head was turned away from the monitor. It looked as if she was going to stick to her decision. While he was all for a woman knowing her own mind, Brighde's stubbornness was infuriating. He knew he was only irritated because she was refusing to agree with him or listen to his point of view and he had enough grace to admit that that was part of the problem, but he was also terrified that he would either run out of time to convince her that he was right or that she was going to go ahead and make a decision without him. He knew she was perfectly entitled to do that but he'd be damned if he was going to make it easy for her.

He looked at her exposed stomach. Her skin was pale and soft. Her stomach flat. She was only twelve weeks along but it was incredible to think that his baby was in there.

His hand shook as he picked up the ultrasound head. He was unbelievably nervous. He'd done hundreds of ultrasounds for all sorts of reasons but he'd never done one where he'd be looking at an image of his own child. It was an incredible moment.

He squeezed the gel onto the machine, flicked the switch and pressed the transducer into Brighde's abdomen. The picture came onto the screen—white stripy muscle fibres, a black womb.

Brighde's head remained turned away from him although he'd angled the screen so she couldn't have seen even if she wanted to. He moved the ultrasound around as he searched for the baby.

There! He felt a goofy smile spread across his

face. That was his child. His trained eye took in the details. At twelve weeks the shape of a little person was easily identifiable. The foetus was about two inches long and he could see the head and body as well as four limbs. It looked perfect.

He moved the head of the ultrasound lower, trying to see if he could change the angle and see the baby in profile. He lost the picture and had to search again. The baby had changed position. Flipping itself around to face the opposite direction. Or had it?

He frowned and moved the transducer head higher again. It took him a moment to figure out what he was seeing.

Brighde could feel Xavier moving the ultrasound over her belly. He was stopping and starting as if he was having trouble getting a clear view. Or looking for something. She started to worry. She'd seen hundreds of ultrasounds. She knew the routine and he seemed to be having trouble making sense of things. Was he having trouble getting a good view? Was something the matter? She was getting nervous.

She turned her head to look at him. 'What is it? What's wrong?'

'Nothing.'

She still couldn't see the screen but she could see Xavier's face. He was smiling. He didn't look worried.

'What is it?' she asked. 'What are you looking at?'

He was looking at her now and she could see tears in his eyes.

Brighde's heart was in her throat. Why was he crying? What was wrong with her baby? 'Tell me,' she insisted. 'What's the matter?'

Xavier shook his head but the wide grin remained. 'It's twins,' he said.

'*Twins?* Are you sure?'

'Absolutely. I can see two sacs and two heartbeats.'

'I want to see,' Brighde said. She couldn't resist looking now. She'd been hoping that the ultrasound would show nothing, that it would tell her the pregnancy test had been a false positive. She'd known that was a long shot—she'd done three pregnancy tests now and all three had returned a positive result—but she had still held on to that hope. But now that the ultrasound had confirmed the pregnancy she had to see for herself.

'You do?'

She nodded and Xavier turned the screen to face her. The screen was black. He moved the transducer head around, pressing on her stomach.

'There. Twin A.'

Brighde caught her breath. She was tiny and perfect.

Xavier pressed a couple of buttons and Brighde could hear the printer spitting out a picture. She wanted to ask him for one for her as well but she couldn't bring herself to ask the question. If she wasn't going to keep the baby did she really want a reminder of her decision?

Xavier was moving the transducer head again

and the image disappeared briefly before another one took its place.

'There's Twin B.'

A carbon copy of the first appeared on the screen.

She could hear Xavier clicking buttons again as the printer whirred in the background but she couldn't take her eyes from the screen. She could see the little flicker of a tiny heart beating.

'Can I hear the heartbeats?' she asked.

Xavier turned on the speakers and the thump-thump of two little hearts echoed in the room. It was the most beautiful sound she'd ever heard.

She blinked back tears.

She was pregnant with twins.

'They look perfect,' Xavier said.

She nodded. They did. But she knew looks could be deceiving. The babies might look perfect on the outside but that was no guarantee. There were no physical signs of Huntington's Disease until much later in life. Who knew what terrible gift she might have passed on to her babies? How was she going to fix this? Now that she'd seen her babies—both of them—the decision to terminate was going to be almost impossible but she was still afraid.

She was afraid to ask the questions. Did she have the gene? Did her babies?

She was scared of the answers and of what the answers might mean.

Being in a state of denial was preferable but was it too late for that now? This was *exactly* why she didn't want to know her status. She didn't want to deal with her own mortality or make tough decisions. It was better not to know. Ignorance was bliss.

She couldn't stay in that state any longer. She knew that.

But what were the chances that she would have escaped inheriting the mutated gene? Surely either she or Nick must have it. They couldn't both be lucky enough to escape.

It was better when they'd both been oblivious. If she hadn't escaped she didn't want to be talked out of the termination. But she knew she had until twenty-four weeks. She had some time. Maybe she could hold on a little longer. Pretend everything was normal, live in denial and enjoy being pregnant.

But she worried that the longer she took the harder the decision would become.

Brighde hesitated at the door to the hospital nursery. She needed to collect a baby to take to her mother but through the glass she could see Xavier. He was standing by a crib, holding a newborn, and Brighde was certain it was the one she was coming for.

She'd avoided him for twenty-four hours. Since the ultrasound. They hadn't discussed it. She needed time to work out what she was going to do and she suspected that Xavier hoped the ultrasound would make her change her mind. She hadn't changed it yet but she was wavering. And she couldn't handle any increased pressure, however subtle, from him. She was barely holding things together without throwing additional emotion into the mix.

She took a minute to watch him holding the baby. He hadn't seen her; he was too caught up in the moment. The baby was clutching his finger and looking up at him, no doubt transfixed by his mesmerising eyes. Seemed like he had the same effect on females of all ages. His lips were moving as he held a one-sided conversation with the baby. He cradled the baby like an expert and she could just imagine him with his own child. He looked utterly gorgeous.

God, she wished things were different.

She shook her head as she punched in the access code and pushed open the door. There wasn't really any room in her head for what-ifs.

'What are you doing in here?' she asked him. There was normally no reason for him to be in the nursery and she hadn't seen him there before.

'Just a quick visit to see how my deliveries are faring. I know they're not my responsibility any more but I like to know how they're going and Shadow here was a bit grizzly so I thought I'd see if I could quieten her down.'

'I've come to take her to her mum,' Brighde said.

'Can you ask her what they were thinking, naming her Shadow?' he asked. 'I can't say I've heard that one before.' He smiled and her heart pounded in her chest, beating frantically like it always seemed to whenever he was near.

'It's not the worst name we've heard,' she replied. She'd seen or heard of many more ridiculous names than Shadow. 'And at least people will be able to spell it,' she added. She'd always hated the fact that no one could spell her name.

Xavier bent over and put his lips to her ear. Brighde's skin tingled as he started to whisper. 'I think we should stick to something simple for our children, like Mary and James.'

Brighde hadn't changed her mind about the fate of her pregnancy but she liked the way 'our children' sounded on Xavier's lips, though she wasn't about to admit that to him.

She knew he wanted kids. Could she really deprive him?

As long as the risks were still there, she knew she could and would. She would much rather deprive him than have him suffer the agony of watching his child die before him.

She locked her gaze onto his. 'Xavier, nothing has changed. Not the risk and not my mind. I can't give you what you want.'

She could work with him professionally—at the moment she didn't have a choice—but there could never be anything personal between them. He wanted things she couldn't give him. It would never work.

She reached out and took the baby from his arms, using Shadow as a shield to separate them in distance while she willed herself to stay strong and reasonable. 'I'm sorry, Xavier, but this would never work.'

She needed to leave now. She needed to get away from the pain she could see in his eyes. She hated knowing that she was hurting him. That she was potentially taking away something he cherished, but the pain now would be nothing compared to the pain later if his children had inherited the mutated gene.

She turned around, leaving him standing there empty-handed. She felt as if she was taking his dream away as she left the nursery but she had no other option. He didn't realise how easily his dream could become a nightmare. She was doing this to protect him. To protect them both.

Her way was still the best way.

The only way.

'Brighde Campbell?'

Brighde glanced at Sarah as the receptionist called her name. Xavier had offered to accompany her to her obstetrics appointment but Brighde didn't want him there. She deliberately hadn't told him when it was. She didn't need someone with a different opinion or agenda to her clouding the issue. She was confused enough already. It was important to her to retain control of the situation but she'd needed some moral support and, besides her brother,

Sarah understood what she was going through better than anyone.

She had made an appointment with Julie Stewart. She'd worked with Julie many times and liked her skills and manner. She needed someone calm and unflappable who she hoped would listen to her concerns and help her through this difficult and confusing time.

'Do you want me to come in with you?' Sarah asked.

Brighde shook her head. 'No, I'll be okay. It was the waiting part I was worried about.' Brighde hadn't trusted herself to go through with the appointment, but having Sarah to keep her company had stopped her from fretting or fleeing. The rest she needed to do on her own. The rest was up to her, completely her decision, and she needed to be strong and independent and take responsibility for her decision.

'Brighde, congratulations. Fourteen weeks, I see, from Xavier's referral,' Julie said as she welcomed her into her office. 'You don't want to see him for your antenatal care?'

Brighde shook her head. Xavier had written the referral for her but that was the last thing she was going to ask of him. 'No,' she replied. 'He's done enough already. He's the father.'

'I see. He didn't want to come to the appointment today?'

'I didn't ask him to. He knows about the pregnancy,' Brighde added quickly when she saw Julie's expression. She knew that was the next question. 'I just didn't want him here today.'

'I don't need to ask if you've had the pregnancy confirmed.'

'Xavier did an ultrasound. It's twins. Two placentas so we're not sure if they're identical or not.'

'Twins is exciting but, as you know, that can be a little more complicated. However, the first appointment is routine either way.'

'It's not quite as routine as you might hope. There's some family history I need to talk to you about. A genetic abnormality.'

'What are we talking about here? Cystic fibrosis? Down Syndrome?'

'No.' Brighde shook her head. 'My mum had Huntington's Disease.'

'Your mum?'

Brighde nodded.

'But not you?'

'I don't know,' she admitted. 'I haven't been tested.'

'Do you want to get tested? I would need to refer you to a genetic counsellor.'

'I want to discuss a termination.' Brighde tried to stay strong. And focused. But she could hear the slight waver in her voice as she tried not to think of the two tiny life-forms growing inside her. She hoped Julie didn't pick up on it. Her hand itched to rest on her belly. A protective gesture and one she resisted. Her body was at war with her mind but she needed to stay resolute.

'Have you discussed this with Xavier?'

'I have. He knows about the Huntington's and he knows my thoughts but, as I understand it, I don't need his permission.'

'That is correct.'

'I don't want to take a chance that either my children or I could develop Huntington's. I've seen what it does. I've lived through it with my mum and I know I couldn't go through it again. I don't plan on letting it take my life if the worst comes to the worst and I don't want to put my family through that, nor do I want to see my family suffer the same fate.'

'Well, the simple answer is yes, I can arrange a termination. We'll need to do an ultrasound scan so I can confirm your dates but we have until twenty-four weeks' gestation. It's better to do these things as early as possible. After that you would need to get a second specialist to support my recommendation. It's a big decision and I want to know that you've considered all options. I'd like you to have an appointment with a psychologist prior to scheduling a termination, if that is what you decide on. I insist on that for all my patients. You have some time so I'd like you to think about it and call me after you've seen the psychologist to schedule a time, if that's still what you want to do. But if you change your mind and want me to organise a referral to the genetic counsellor that's fine too. The other alternative is testing the foetuses. I can do an amniocentesis if you choose.'

'No. I don't want that. If one of the babies tests positive then I'll know my prognosis too.'

'Fair enough,' Julie replied as she handed her a card with the psychologist's details on it. 'Call me or schedule another appointment once you've seen the psychologist, okay?'

Brighde took the card as she agreed with Julie's conditions. She needed to get out of there. She needed to think.

'How did it go?' Sarah asked when Brighde reappeared.

'I'm not sure.'

She waited until they had left the rooms. This was not a conversation she wanted to have within earshot of any other mothers or pregnant women.

'Julie will perform the termination if I want her to but she insists on an appointment with a psychologist first.'

'That makes sense.'

'Am I doing the right thing? What if the babies are perfectly fine?'

'Only you can make that decision, Brighde.'

'I spoke to Nick and Imogen about testing the other day.'

'Are you thinking about it too?'

'I still don't know but the fact that I even want to talk about it worries me. I'm second-guessing myself now. I was always so sure, so convinced that I would never have children and everything has changed overnight. Nick and I spent so many years being adamant that we wouldn't get tested. I understand why Nick changed his mind but I wanted to know what they would have done if he'd tested positive. I wanted to know if Nick would still marry Imogen, knowing what we went through with Mum. Whether he would have been prepared to put Immy through that.'

'And what did he say?'

'He said no. Which was what we always thought, and that's effectively where I stand too, but Imogen said yes. She said they would still get married but they would have done pre-implantation genetic testing done on any embryos to make sure they didn't inherit the mutation. I can see her point of view but I don't have that option. I'm already pregnant.'

'But you could test the babies. An amnio would tell you what you need to know, right?'

'Yes. But it might also tell me my fate, one way or the other, and I'm not sure if I'm ready to know that.'

'Brighde, if I'm honest, this is about more than just you now. I understood your reasons for not getting tested but this isn't just about you any more. I know you're battling with this decision and you need to ask yourself why. I know you're scared but I also know you want these babies. You have to find out what you're dealing with. You need some answers so you can make decisions with a clear conscience. I know it's hard but we will support you, Nick, Imogen and me.'

She noticed that Sarah hadn't mentioned

Xavier. Did she presume he wouldn't support her decision?

But Sarah was right. She couldn't in good conscience go through with a termination without all the facts. She put the psychologist's business card in her pocket. She would save that number for later. She had another decision to make first. Who should she test? Herself or her babies?

Brighde switched her phone on as handover finished and her shift officially ended and saw two missed calls from the same number. The number wasn't programmed into her phone but she recognised it instantly. It was the genetic counsellor's number.

It had been three weeks since she'd called her obstetrician and asked for a referral to the genetic counsellor and two weeks since she'd had blood taken for the test. The counsellor had promised to get the results rushed through. The results must be in. This was it.

She saw Xavier walking along the corridor and felt the blood rush from her head. She wasn't ready for this.

She was vaguely aware of darkness swirling at the edges of her vision and she could feel the floor rising up to meet her as the room started to spin. She reached for the desk, trying to steady the room, to steady herself, but her hand found only thin air.

'Brighde!' She heard Xavier's voice. He sounded miles away.

'Brighde?'

She opened her eyes to find herself in Xavier's arms, pressed against his chest, as he carried her along the corridor.

How did she get there? 'What happened? What are you doing?'

'You fainted.'

'Fainted?' She wasn't a fainter. 'Where are we going?' she asked as he pushed open a door to an examination room.

'To check you out,' he said as he laid her on the bed and reached for the blood pressure cuff.

He wrapped it around her arm and she watched his long fingers fix it in place.

She wanted to sit up. She felt perfectly fine but something must have happened. Something must have triggered the fainting spell. She lay still and tried to remember what had happened. The counsellor!

The blood pressure machine beeped and the monitor showed one-ten over seventy. 'That's a little low.'

'It's normal for me,' she told him.

'Is fainting normal too?'

'No.'

'Then we should find out what caused it.'

'I know what caused it,' she said as she patted her pocket. 'Where's my phone?'

'Here.' He pulled it from the pocket of his trousers and handed it to her. 'What's so important?'

Brighde's hand shook as she took her phone from him. 'I saw a genetic counsellor a couple of weeks ago. I had blood tests done.' She swiped the screen as she spoke; she couldn't bring herself to look at him.

'Why didn't you tell me?' She could hear the hurt and confusion in his voice. The one thing he'd been asking her to do and she'd done it behind his back.

'I didn't tell anyone,' she explained. 'I thought it would make the wait worse if other people were also expecting news.' And she didn't think she was strong enough to handle the weight of expectation. If no one else knew, she could pretend for a little longer. And she didn't want to answer questions until she had the results. 'I didn't want to make any promises I couldn't keep. I just got a message on my phone. The test results must be back.'

'What did the message say?'

'I don't know. I haven't listened to it yet. That's what I was doing when I fainted.' She hit voicemail and held the phone to her ear.

'Do you want me to wait outside?'

She shook her head. She thought she might chicken out if left on her own. Xavier's presence was the catalyst she needed to listen to the message. His calm demeanour and physical size gave her a sense of strength she didn't have if left to her own devices.

'He wants me to go in to his office,' she said as she ended the call. 'He's there until six o'clock today.'

'Is that all he said?'

She nodded, knowing what Xavier was asking. 'He won't open the results until I'm there.'

'Where is his office?'

'South Melbourne.'

'I suppose you want to catch the tram,' Xavier said but his tone was teasing and there was warmth in his dark brown eyes. 'Would you like me to drive you?'

'I don't know if I'm going to go yet. I'm not sure I'm ready to hear what he has to say.'

'Brighde, I know this must be daunting for you. Just making the decision to get tested must have been difficult and I understand if you need more time but you don't have to go alone. I imagine the suggestion was made to bring someone with you?' He waited while she nodded. 'I can do that for you. No pressure. Just a friendly face. Someone to hold your hand.'

She didn't want to go on her own. She knew she wouldn't cope. She could ask Sarah to go with her but she wanted Xavier. She felt safe with him. She wanted to be back in his arms. She wished she could stay there for ever and she wished she could make everything else go away. She wished she could be normal. They might not have a future together but she needed him with her just for now.

And besides, if Xavier heard the results it might be easier to persuade him that she was right. She felt bad that she couldn't give him what he wanted but maybe letting him accompany her would make up for that somehow.

Xavier noted that Brighde introduced him to the counsellor only as a friend, not as the father of her twins. It seemed she was determined to keep him at arm's length. He supposed he should be thankful that she'd allowed him to accompany her for this meeting even if he obviously still wasn't going to be asked for his opinion. He wondered what it would take to get her to let him into her life properly. He was determined to be a part of it; she had got him thinking about the future, imagining a life with his children and with her. Very definitely with her. She was stubborn but fragile, independent but wounded and he wanted to take care of her. He wanted to give her peace and security, even though he knew that might be out of his control. She brought out all his protective instincts and he wanted her to feel protected and cherished. But he knew he had some work to do if he was going to convince her that he should be part of her life. She was so set on shutting him out.

'How much has Brighde explained to you about testing?' Tuan asked after the introductions had been made.

'Not a lot,' Xavier replied. Although the honest answer would have been 'nothing'. If he'd known Brighde was being tested he would have done his research. He hated being unprepared.

He'd done a bit of background reading on the disease early on, trying to get inside Brighde's head, trying to understand her thought processes, but he hadn't spent a lot of time on the science of the testing procedure. 'I am an obstetrician so I'll understand the facts, but Huntington's Disease is not something I've had first-hand experience with.'

'All right then. I'll just explain what we are looking for in the testing process. Huntington's Disease is caused by a mutation in the HTT gene which is instrumental in making the Huntingtin protein. The faulty gene produces an oversized version of the protein which builds up in the brain and attacks the neurons, causing the symptoms we see in Huntington's Disease. We still don't know why the faulty gene only attacks the nerves in the brain but that's what happens. In order to determine whether an individual is likely to develop Huntington's Disease we need to count the number of CAG trinucleotide repeats. Normally a CAG segment is repeated between ten and thirty-five times within the Huntingtin gene. In people who are going to develop Huntington's Disease the number of repeats will be anything in the range of forty to more than one hundred and twenty. Thirty-six to thirty-nine repeats is considered the grey area where individuals *may* develop the disease.'

Tuan's desk was clear except for a single white envelope. He reached for the envelope and picked it up, looking at Brighde. 'These are your test results. Do you have any questions before we open it?'

'We're hoping for a number less than thirty-six?' she checked. She knew that her brother's tests had shown ten repeats and that had been good news but she had never bothered to investigate further than that. She was still of the opinion that ignorance was bliss.

'For you to test negative, that's right. Have you thought about what you will do if the test is positive?'

Brighde nodded. 'If I have Huntington's Disease I will terminate the pregnancy.'

'You understand that even if you test positive the babies could still be fine? They may both have inherited the healthy gene.'

Brighde understood exactly what Tuan was telling her. Which was that if she tested positive but didn't test the babies she wouldn't know their fate for certain; therefore, she could be terminating perfectly healthy foetuses. She got that, but this wasn't something she was prepared to negotiate. Huntington's was a genetically dominant disease. If Brighde tested positive the chances of both babies escaping the mutation was not impossible but it was improbable.

'Yes. But I watched my mother die and it was the worst thing imaginable. If I have the disease I don't want to put my own children through that. And I won't.'

'All right,' Tuan continued. 'It's not my job to tell you what to do; it's my job to give you the facts. Are you ready?'

Brighde looked at Xavier. She was terrified but it was time to find out.

He squeezed her hand and she looked back

at Tuan and nodded. He slit open the envelope and pulled out a single piece of paper.

The piece of paper that would determine her future and possibly that of her unborn children too. It didn't look important enough to Brighde.

She held her breath.

'You have twenty-nine repeats.'

Brighde breathed a sigh of relief. Tears came to her eyes. She couldn't believe it. 'I'm going to be okay?' She and Nick had *both* had a win in the genetic lottery? She was safe. She'd dodged a bullet. It was hard to comprehend; she'd been so certain her test would be positive. She hadn't dared let herself believe her result could be anything else. How could they both be so lucky?

Her hands and her knees were shaking. Adrenalin coursed through her. Fear was replaced with relief, leaving her light-headed. She took a deep breath. 'So I won't develop HD?'

'That's right.' Brighde felt like bursting into tears of relief. '*You* won't develop HD…'

She could hear a *but* in Tuan's voice. Why was there a *but*? She'd tested negative. She was going to be okay. She frowned. 'Is there more?' she questioned him. 'What aren't you telling me?'

'Fewer than thirty-six repeats means that you won't develop the disease but there's a range termed the unstable range.'

'Which is what?' Her voice shook. Fear was back.

'Between twenty-seven and thirty-five repeats.'

'And I'm in there? The unstable range?'

Tuan nodded.

'And what does that mean?' Xavier asked.

'It means things can be a little ambiguous.'

Brighde didn't like the sound of that at all. What did Tuan know that she didn't? She could feel herself starting to panic. Xavier was still holding her hand and she was squeezing his fingers so hard she feared she would cut off his circulation but he wasn't flinching.

'It means you won't develop HD,' Tuan continued. Brighde watched his lips carefully. He sounded as though he was speaking underwater;

she knew it was because her brain was fuzzy, and she had to concentrate hard to make sense of what he was telling her. 'But there's a possibility that the CAG gene could expand when passed from a parent to a child.'

Her fainting spell had passed but she now thought she might vomit as Tuan's explanation sunk in. 'Are you telling me I won't develop HD but my children might?'

CHAPTER SEVEN

BRIGHDE STARED AT TUAN. 'So, I'm safe but the babies might not be? I might still have passed on a faulty gene?'

'It's more likely that the gene could continue to expand when the gene is passed through the father's side. We're not certain about the mother.'

'But you don't know for sure?'

Brighde fought back tears. The test results hadn't helped at all. They had made things worse, not better, and given her more questions than answers.

Tuan was shaking his head. 'No. I'm sorry.'

Xavier started to speak but Brighde held up her hand. 'Stop.' She couldn't look at him. She was seconds away from bursting into tears, from losing her composure completely and she knew that if she looked at Xavier and saw compassion or concern in his eyes she wouldn't be able to maintain her composure. She needed to think. She couldn't afford to go to pieces. 'I need a moment.'

She wasn't coping. Not at all. This was even worse than she'd imagined. She'd been prepared to hear that she had the mutation but to learn that she would be okay but she might have condemned her unborn babies was devastating. She'd chosen not to test the babies since it might have given her an insight into her own future anyway. If one of the babies had tested positive it would have confirmed that she carried the gene. But to find out she might have passed on the gene *without* testing positive herself—that she hadn't expected and she wasn't sure how to deal with it.

She took a deep breath and kept her eyes fixed on Tuan. 'What do I do now?' In her mind, it was still a question of her options. The decisions were still all hers. This was her family's legacy; Xavier was just a bystander.

'That's up to you,' Tuan replied. 'You can test the foetuses or terminate the pregnancy. The only way to know for sure is to have an amniocentesis but the choice is yours. You've got time. You have got until twenty-four weeks before a termination gets complicated but you need to make sure you're okay with whatever decision you make.' Tuan stood up from behind his desk. 'You'll need some time to process this. You're welcome to stay in here for as long as you need and if you want any more information or would like to discuss anything further, today or in the future, I'm available. I really am sorry.'

He left them alone. Brighde knew she was in shock. Xavier was silent too; she supposed the shock was just as great for him. Worse, maybe. She'd always expected that she would have the repeat so she should have anticipated bad news. But to hear what she thought was good news and then to have it tainted by premonitions of disaster was almost more than she could bear.

'Are you okay?' he asked.

'No. I'm definitely not okay.'

'You didn't know the significance in the different numbers of repeats?'

'No. I knew nothing about unstable ranges or grey areas.' She'd never researched testing as she'd never intended to get tested. She'd preferred to live in a state of denial.

What had she done to her babies?

Her hand was resting on her stomach. An unconscious, protective gesture she'd found herself making more and more often.

She dropped her head, imagining for a moment that she'd be able to see her babies. What would she tell them?

I'm so sorry. I never meant to hurt you.

I never meant to have you.

But now that she was pregnant she knew she couldn't terminate the pregnancy without knowing what hand she'd dealt them.

Everything had changed yet again. If the twins had escaped the mutation then everything was good. She would be around to see her children grow up. But if they hadn't she would have to go ahead with a termination. She couldn't stand the thought of passing on the faulty gene. She couldn't do that to her own children.

She felt Xavier's fingers under her chin. He lifted her head and she could see the worry in his dark eyes. Was it her worry reflecting back at her or was he just as concerned?

His thumb brushed across her cheek and she could feel dampness on her skin. She hadn't been aware that she was crying but now she could feel the tears gathering on her bottom lashes and spilling over onto her cheeks.

'I'll take you home,' Xavier said.

She nodded mutely. She just wanted to curl up in a ball in her bed in the darkness and wait for this all to go away. She hadn't prepared herself for this news at all and it was overwhelming. She didn't know if she was strong enough to cope with the decisions that she still faced.

Xavier's phone rang just as he pulled up in front of her house. He'd been silent on the drive home and Brighde was grateful. She didn't feel like talking. She didn't think she was capable of holding a conversation. Her brain wasn't holding any thoughts at all. It kept jumping from one thought to another. She was completely unsettled.

She climbed out of the car and walked up the path. Xavier followed her up the path, talking on his phone.

'Is Sarah home?' he asked as she unlocked the front door.

'No. She's working a late. Why?'

'That was the hospital. One of my patients is in labour. I should go but if you like I can call someone to cover me so I can stay with you.'

'No. I'm fine,' she lied. She wasn't fine but she didn't know if she wanted company. She just wanted to be left alone with the consequences of her actions and her grief.

She wanted everything to go back to normal.

'Is there someone else who can come and stay with you? I don't think you should be alone. What about your brother?'

Brighde shook her head. 'No. I'm okay.' She still hadn't told Nick she was pregnant and she wasn't about to tell him today. Definitely not today. 'It's all right. Go.'

Brighde had a restless night's sleep. She dreamt in vivid Technicolor. Disturbing dreams. She finally fell asleep again as Saturday dawned, only to be woken later by a knock on the front door. She waited to see if Sarah would answer before remembering that she'd been doing a late/early and would already be back at work.

She stumbled out of bed and pulled her curtains back at the corner, craning her head to see who was disturbing her.

Xavier.

'What are you doing here?' she asked as she opened the door. Was he checking on her or the babies? Worried about her or only about them?

'I came to see how you are. Whether there's anything you need.'

She shook her head as she stepped aside to let him in. She couldn't stand in the doorway dressed in nothing but an old T-shirt. 'I'm fine.'

The expression on Xavier's face told her he didn't believe her but he didn't argue.

'In that case I have a suggestion.'

'What is it?'

'How would you like to get away for the weekend?'

'Why?'

'Why not? I know Sarah is working this weekend. Which means you'll be home alone. I don't want you staring at the walls and worrying.'

'Maybe I want to be alone,' she grumbled.

'If you won't listen to me, would you listen to my sister? I've learnt that in order to live a stress-free life it's wise to listen to her. She suggested that a change of scenery might be good therapy. Please, won't you give it a shot? Twenty-four hours, that's all I'm asking for.'

What else had she planned for the next twenty-four hours? Nothing at all. He was right. She would just sit and fret. She sighed. 'What do I need?'

Xavier grinned and her spirits lifted instantly. She could think of worse ways to spend the next day than in his company. 'Walking shoes, a warm coat. Something a little smart for dinner and a smile.'

'Where are we going?'

'That's a surprise.'

'Brighde? We're here.'

Xavier's voice roused her from sleep. She hadn't been able to keep her eyes open once they'd hit the highway out of Melbourne; the steady thrum of the car engine had lulled her to sleep and she still had no idea where Xavier had taken her.

'Welcome to Daylesford.'

'Spa country?'

Daylesford was famous for its mineral springs, spa retreats, restaurants and natural beauty and it was putting on a magnificent display today, Brighde thought as Xavier drove through the picturesque country town. She'd heard about the area but never visited. It looked spectacular. The myriad trees showed off their autumn colours. Gold, fiery red, burnt orange, a touch of green against a crisp, clean blue sky. It was one of those beautiful Victorian days when the weather was being kind and anything seemed possible.

Xavier turned off the road into their accommodation that sat on the edge of the lake. Brighde had heard about this five-star restaurant and hotel. 'Are we staying here?'

'As long as you've got no objections,' Xavier said as he switched off the engine. He smiled at her and Brighde's stomach flipped.

He jumped out of the car while Brighde sat for a moment to gather her thoughts. This wasn't a romantic couple's weekend away; this was Xavier's version of R&R. He'd promised to give her time and space to rest and recover but she couldn't afford to let her guard down. She needed to keep her wits about her and remember what was at stake. She still had some decisions to make. Big decisions. And she couldn't get too comfortable with Xavier as it was more than likely that her decisions would destroy any chance they might have had at any sort of relationship.

'Are you hungry?' Xavier opened Brighde's door and reached for her hand. She took his hand without thinking; it was warm and large and reassuring and his touch sent her stomach tumbling again.

She wasn't hungry or tired. She was restless. She had to move. Had to get busy. Had to get her mind off Xavier and his smile, his come-to-bed eyes and his warm hands and how he made her feel. Maybe it was the pregnancy hormones but she was feeling very much like ripping his clothes off.

'Not really.' She was dying to see their room—she wondered if he'd booked one or two—but she could see the lake from the car park and it looked so peaceful and serene and it called to her. 'After we check in I might go for a walk.'

Xavier checked them in—just the one room, she noted—and they followed the porter.

The door swung open to reveal a light-filled space with views of the lake through expansive windows set either side of a pair of French windows. The king-size bed had a plush bedhead upholstered in a black and white fabric, the bathroom was as big as her kitchen with a bath the size of her dining table and a couch was positioned in front of the window to catch the view but also angled towards a gas fire. The black and white theme continued in the soft furnishings of the room and into the bathroom with hints of gold. Brighde had never seen anything as luxurious as this suite.

She spun around slowly, taking it all in. 'Wow! This is gorgeous.'

'You like it?' Xavier asked as he tipped the porter.

'It's amazing.'

'I didn't intend to book just one room—it was all they had left at short notice but I thought you could have the bed and I'll take the couch.'

Brighde looked at the couch. It looked comfortable but not nearly long enough to accommodate Xavier's six-feet, two-inch frame. She would offer him the bed but she'd leave that discussion for later; she knew he wouldn't accept now. 'Are you sure?'

'Positive. This weekend is all about giving you a chance to recharge. I want you to have a good night's sleep.'

Sleep was the last thing on Brighde's mind. The first thing wasn't wise though so she went for option two.

'I think I'll go for a walk around the lake while the weather holds,' she said. The Victorian weather was notoriously fickle and locals learnt to take advantage of clear skies whenever possible. The weather could change in an instant. 'Would you like to come?'

They were able to step out through the French windows onto a small deck from where stairs led down onto the lakeside path. The gardens were planted with Australian natives and Brighde could hear frogs croaking in the reeds and a kookaburra laughing in the distance. She wasn't watching where she was walking, mesmerised by her surroundings, and she missed the bottom step, stumbling slightly. Xavier grabbed her hand, preventing her from falling, and he didn't let go even as she recovered her feet. Brighde wondered if she should pull her hand away but it felt so good she decided not to make a fuss. Her body was flooded with pregnancy hormones, which made it difficult to think straight. Her brain felt like complete mush at times while at other times she was so sexually charged she couldn't think about anything else. But it was strange how those times only occurred whenever Xavier was near.

They walked in silence and Brighde savoured the peace and the sensation of having her hand in Xavier's. Her situation could be so perfect if it wasn't built on mistakes and haunted by her fears.

'Was this really your sister's idea?'

She was curious to know what Xavier had told her family about her. She liked the idea that they knew about her. It meant she existed in his life.

Did she want that?

She did but she doubted she'd get what she

wanted. That would be too much to ask for and she'd learned not to ask for, or expect, too much.

For the moment, it was enough to know that she was free of the possibility of inheriting HD. That was good news and she needed to remember to cherish that outcome. Could she dare to hope that both her babies had also been spared? If they hadn't then she and Xavier didn't stand a chance.

'She suggested the change of scenery. I chose the location.'

'You've done well,' Brighde said as she watched a pair of black swans glide serenely past them on the lake. 'Which sister was it?'

'Mary. She's the eldest and the bossiest. It's good to let her get her way occasionally and I think she got it right today.'

'What about the others?' Brighde was enjoying the chance to talk about someone else's family for a change. Hearing about his life meant she didn't have to think about hers.

'Eve is number two. She's not quite as serious as Mary. A bit more of a free spirit. She's pregnant with her third child; Mary has four. Then, Angie and Gabby, the twins, are younger than me.'

'You have twin sisters?' Brighde was surprised that he hadn't mentioned that before.

He nodded.

'Why haven't you told me about them?'

'Would it make any difference?'

'I guess not.' It was irrelevant to her situation, she supposed, but it felt like another connection to his family and she liked that idea. 'But what was it like having twins in the family?'

'Awful,' he said but he was grinning. He really was irresistible when he smiled. 'I was four when they were born and they made my life hell.'

'Did they really?'

'Of course. But I adore them. Now. But I imagine they were hard work to begin with. I'm sure my mum would happily pass on any words of advice about raising twins if you're interested.'

Brighde wasn't sure she was ready to go there.

Either to meet his mum or to talk about raising twins. That would be admitting that she was going ahead with the pregnancy.

When she didn't reply he continued. 'I just remember a lot of bottles and nappies and crying. I can't say I'm an expert on raising kids but I'm getting plenty of practice with my sisters' tribes.'

'You've got eight nieces and nephews, you said?'

'Yep, plus one on the way and a couple of godchildren as well.'

'That sounds busy,' she said as she wrapped her scarf around her neck a little more tightly. They had reached the far side of the lake and the wind was blowing more steadily on this side and there was a bit of a chill in the autumn air.

'It is,' he said as they approached a picturesque red-roofed weatherboard kiosk. 'Shall I get us both something hot to drink?' he asked, leading her onto the deck of the kiosk that extended out over the lake. 'Would you like to sit inside or out?'

A row of brightly coloured paddleboats was tied to the bank and several had been rented and were drifting on the water. Despite the wind, the views were pretty. 'Outside, I think.'

Xavier found a table and chairs on the deck that was partly sheltered from the elements. Brighde sat and thought about his large family as she waited for him to return with their drinks. His family sounded close and she tried to imagine her babies with a heap of cousins. She and Nick only had each other. Their parents had both been only children but her babies would have cousins on both sides *and* of similar age. She wondered what her family would think about this whole situation. What would her mum have thought of Xavier? What she would have said if she'd known Nick and Brighde were both going to give her grandchildren.

Xavier put Brighde's hot chocolate on the table but she didn't acknowledge his return. She was gazing across the lake, lost in her thoughts. But she didn't look relaxed. She looked like she had the weight of the world on her shoulders. He'd brought her here hoping to give her a chance to relax, rest and replenish her reserves. He knew she wouldn't be able to make sensible decisions if she was exhausted and emotional. He knew she hadn't been sleeping well. Sarah had mentioned it but he could see it in her face. She'd lost weight and had dark circles under her eyes. Her energy seemed to have been extinguished and she'd lost some of her spark. Seeing her like this made him feel terrible. He'd done this to her. He'd put her in this position.

But there was some good news in all of this. She had tested negative. She was going to be okay.

That should be one less concern for her but he knew she was still stressed about what she might have inflicted on their children. He'd hoped that bringing her to Daylesford would help to get her mind off that. It had to be better than leaving her home alone, with only her thoughts for company. He didn't want to put any pressure on her but he'd hoped a change of environment might allow her to forget her worries and fears. Even a temporary reprieve had to be a good thing, but it didn't look as though his plan was working.

'Is everything okay?'

She jumped in her chair. 'Sorry, what did you say?'

'I asked if you were okay.'

'Yes, I'm fine.'

'If you want to talk I'm a good listener. My sisters have taught me that as well. Whether by accident or design, I'm not sure, but they talked so much it was always hard to get a word in so I learnt to listen.'

He was rewarded with a smile. Her smile was fantastic. Wide and sincere. Although this one didn't quite reach her eyes. What was on her mind?

'I was just thinking about my mum. Wondering what she would think of my situation. And what she would do.'

'What do you think she would do?'

'I don't know. I guess her situation was completely different to mine. Things have changed so much since I was born. Not in terms of any treatment for HD but in terms of the genetic testing. Almost all the worthwhile discoveries about the disease and all the useful advances that have been made have happened since I was born, but none of it is going to help me.'

He begged to differ. The tests that were available today gave them a lot more information than ever before. Information that could be used to make informed decisions. And he was all for that. He still couldn't understand how testing could be a bad idea. Or an idea that wasn't on the table for consideration. But he'd promised that he wouldn't pressure her. This weekend was all about peace.

'The Huntingtin gene wasn't identified until 1983 and genetic testing wasn't an option until 1994, five years after I was born, so by the time Mum could have learned that she was going to develop HD Nick and I were already born. And pre-implantation testing has only been possible since 2003 so Mum didn't have any of the options that are available today, but I still wonder what she would have done if she'd had access to testing. Would she have taken a chance and had a family?'

'You never asked her?'

Brighde shook her head. 'No. We never really spoke about the future. We were too busy trying to survive in the present. I wish I had though—not that it would have changed anything, really. Her only option would have been not to have kids. But it's too late to know now and it's a regret I'll have to live with. I guess I just wonder what advice she'd have had for me.'

'Have you spoken to your brother?'

'No,' she said as she picked up her hot chocolate.

'Why not?' He was curious to know why she hadn't said anything to her family.

'We've had enough bad news in our life. He's happy now. He's getting married and they're expecting their first child. I don't want to take the gloss off their news with my troubles.'

Xavier finished his drink and checked his

watch. 'I made a massage appointment for you,' he said. 'I wasn't sure if you'd like it but there weren't many spots available so I took the liberty. If you'd like it we'd better head back.'

'That sounds fabulous—thank you.' She drained her hot chocolate, leaving a dusting of chocolate powder on her top lip.

He reached across the table and wiped the chocolate from her lip with his thumb. Brighde's blue-grey eyes widened and her pupils dilated and he fought the urge to lean across the table and kiss her soundly.

He wished things were different. Less complicated. He was still prepared to try to work things out but so many of the decisions were Brighde's alone to make. He really didn't have much influence over how things were going to turn out. There was nothing much he could do except to try to show her that he was there to support her and hope for the best. He knew there were no guarantees in life but he didn't doubt that, if Brighde was willing to give him a go, they could have a future together. But it was all up to her.

He stood and held her chair for her and kept her company as they walked back around the lake.

Brighde stretched out on the couch in front of the fire. Housekeeping had been to their room while they were at dinner and had turned down the bed and turned on the fire. The room was lit by lamps and by firelight, casting a warm glow.

Xavier picked up a chocolate that had been left on the pillow by Housekeeping.

'After-dinner chocolate?' he offered.

Brighde groaned. 'I couldn't eat another thing.' Dinner had been divine. Poached pheasant with autumn vegetables, followed by a pear and rhubarb tart. She couldn't remember when she'd had a nicer meal. 'I should go to bed but I don't think I can move.'

'That's my bed, don't forget; you'll have to move at some stage.'

'Come and sit with me.'

Xavier sat on the floor at her feet, leaning his back against the couch. That wasn't what she'd intended. 'That doesn't look very comfortable,' she said as she sat up and shuffled to one side to make some room. 'You can sit up here.'

He sat in the corner of the couch, his long legs stretched out in front of him towards the fire, and pulled Brighde down again so she could lie with her head in his lap. She closed her eyes and breathed out slowly as he stroked her hair.

'Have you had a good day?'

Brighde sighed. 'I've had a great day. Thank you.'

'How are you feeling? Apart from full?'

She felt safe but she wasn't about to share that with him. She wasn't used to revealing her innermost thoughts. 'I'm feeling relieved.'

'About testing negative?'

She rolled onto her back, opened her eyes and looked up at him as she nodded.

'I kind of ignored that yesterday. I was so worried about what still might be that I sort of forgot that Tuan told me I'd be okay. I'd always been so certain that I would test positive so it didn't sink in that the tests were negative. But it's a double-edged sword. On one hand I'm relieved, but if I wasn't pregnant I'd be absolutely ecstatic, not just relieved. But knowing that I still might have inadvertently affected my babies is hard to come to terms with. In a way I think it would have been easier to deal with if I *had* tested positive. But it's ironic, isn't it? If I wasn't pregnant I never would have got tested and I wouldn't have this sense of relief. I've got one answer from the test results but more questions.'

'About the babies?'

'Yes.'

'I know I said I would just listen,' he told her. 'That all decisions were yours, but from a purely medical point of view the sooner you make decisions the better. Particularly regarding a termination.'

'You do agree that a termination is okay in certain cases?' she asked. 'I've been thinking about the ramifications a lot, particularly since delivering the baby with Down Syndrome. There's a difference between that and HD. That child will grow up with the syndrome; they won't know any different, their life will be constant. A child who has the mutated HTT gene will lead a completely normal life for thirty or forty years and that means that when the symptoms start it will be a massive blow. They will lose all normality. That's what worries me. That seems cruel. It *is* cruel. I lived through it with my mother and I can't do it again. I need to know how you feel about that.'

She'd been avoiding asking him direct questions. She'd been making assumptions about what he would say but maybe he had changed his mind. She hadn't asked. But now she was struggling with the decision-making. She didn't want him to feel excluded but she also didn't want to make all the decisions. He'd shown her his support and she felt she needed to show him some consideration.

'I need to know for certain one way or another before I would be happy with a termination,' he replied. 'The babies might be fine and then we're worrying for no good reason. Will you have an amnio to find out?'

She'd been thinking about this. A lot. Her babies might be fine and part of her would love her own happily ever after—a husband, children, a family of her own—but she was still scared. When Xavier was around it was easy to forget all the bad things that could happen and she found herself thinking ahead to the future, daydreaming about falling in love and living a long and happy life. But if she was ever going to get a chance at that she needed to make some decisions and she knew she didn't really have a choice. It wasn't the testing she had to consider now—she knew that was inevitable—it was what would happen next. Whether Xavier would agree with her decisions once they got the results or whether he'd still want her to continue with the pregnancy.

'Would you agree to a termination if the tests came back positive?' she asked. She had to know. She couldn't go ahead with the tests if he would give her grief over her decisions if the tests *were* positive. Legally she didn't need his consent but she wanted his support. They might not agree on everything but he was entitled to his opinion, although, in this case, she was going to do what she believed was best.

'Can I have some time to think about my answer? It's a big decision and I'm just not sure how I feel about the termination when, regardless of the genetic make-up, our babies will be perfectly healthy well into adulthood.'

'Have you ever seen, with your own eyes, someone with late stage Huntington's? Not read about it or watched videos but actually seen for yourself what it does?' she asked.

He shook his head. 'No, I haven't.'

'Then you have no idea what this disease does to someone. Not just the person who has the disease but the entire family. It destroyed ours.' She sat up on the couch and turned to face him, sitting cross-legged on the cushions. She didn't know how to make him understand the horror of this disease. 'You can spend thirty or forty years of your life being perfectly fine and then, one day, your world starts to crumble. Just little things at first, a slight change in your personality or moods, some forgetfulness—things that you probably won't even notice but your family will. And then depression might be the next thing or your motor functions will deteriorate. You'll start to stumble or have trouble holding your knife and fork. Over the next fifteen or twenty years your body and your brain decay and there's nothing you can do.

'Nick and I watched our mother suffer through this. Our father left us to do that alone. I was nine years old when her symptoms started. We did what we could until we couldn't cope any more. When I was twenty we had to put her into full-time care. She was forty-nine when she died. That is too young. Way too young. And the only reason she lived that long was because of us. I think she would have given up long before if it wasn't for us.

'That is why I didn't want to know if I carried the gene. I've seen what it does and it scares me.

It terrifies me. But now I know. And that should be good news but now I'm frightened of what it means for my children. You need to understand what this could mean. I know how much you want children and, believe me, this isn't an easy decision. I would love children too but not if I have passed on a faulty gene.' She shook her head. 'Not Huntington's. It's too awful and I could never forgive myself. You need to understand what it is like.'

'What are you saying?'

'I want you to go and see someone who is suffering with late stage HD and then tell me if you could imagine seeing your own children suffer the same fate. Once you've done that I will agree to an amnio but *only* if you agree, in writing, that the pregnancy should be terminated if the tests are positive. If we don't get them tested while they are in utero then we have no control over anything and I can't have these babies without knowing their fate. And I can't have these babies if the test is positive either. If we don't get the tests done now then once the children are born they would have to wait until they turn eighteen before they could request testing and then, at this stage, if the test is positive there is *still* nothing that can be done. I want you to see what this disease looks like and I need you to remember that, right now, there is no cure. There is no way to stop the suffering.'

CHAPTER EIGHT

XAVIER STOOD IN the car park. He wasn't sure about this. He had agreed to Brighde's request as he couldn't imagine her terminating the pregnancy without doing an amniocentesis. And if he had to visit the care facility in order to meet her terms then he would.

She hadn't offered to accompany him and he hadn't asked her to. He knew she would refuse. She wouldn't want to see the patients here—he'd learnt that denial was her preferred way of coping—but she had given him the address. He wondered if this was where her mum had spent her last days or months or years. He didn't know. There was so much he didn't know. She didn't volunteer a lot and he was reluctant to ask her. He had no idea where he stood within the framework of her life. Did she trust him?

Would she want to confide in him? How did she view him? Did she see him as the enemy? Someone who had gotten her into this position in the first place? Someone who wanted a different outcome from her? Was there a chance she could see him as someone permanent in her life or was she eager to cut him out of her life as quickly as possible? Would seeing him always remind her of this situation she was in? This awkward, unwanted situation? How did she feel about him? How did he feel about her?

There were far too many questions to tackle at the moment. He'd take one step at a time and the first step, before it was too late, was to try to convince Brighde to find out exactly what they were dealing with. To find out exactly what situation they were in. He didn't want to play guessing games and if he needed answers he needed to go inside the building. From the outside it looked harmless enough, ordinary even—a two-storey brick building, surrounded by gum trees. He could hear birds chattering and water flowing.

He was nervous but he couldn't stand outside all day. He headed for the front entrance. A fountain bubbled in front of the building. From the outside everything seemed calm and peaceful. In complete contrast to how he was feeling.

An elderly woman staffed the reception desk. Xavier hadn't really thought of how he was going to explain his visit here but he'd been hoping for a younger staff member. In his experience they were less likely to question his motives once they knew he was a doctor and, if he was honest, a young female employee wouldn't hesitate to let him have his way when it came to work.

'Good morning.' He flashed his best smile, deciding against the full charm offensive. He needed to present himself as a professional. That was the angle he was going to use. He pulled his identification from his wallet, his driver's licence and business card, and slid them onto the desk. 'My name is Dr O'Donnell; I was wondering if there was someone I could speak to regarding Huntington's Disease.'

The woman, who according to her badge was named Joyce, studied his ID before returning it to him. She looked up. 'What is it you want to know?'

'I'm an obstetrician and I have a patient who is pregnant and the baby has tested positive for Huntington's Disease.' He'd stretched the truth marginally but refused to feel guilty about a slight exaggeration of the facts. They were mostly accurate. 'She is considering a termination and I really don't have much idea about the disease and what she's dealing with. I'd like to get a better understanding of the condition.'

'You need to see Dr Baird,' came the reply, 'but she's not here at the moment. We don't have doctors on site. Would you like me to take your details and pass them on to her?'

Did he? He really wanted to see some of the patients. That was the task Brighde had set him. 'Is there someone else I could talk to while I'm here, one of the nursing staff maybe?'

Joyce frowned. 'I'm not sure,' she said. 'I'd have to check with the manager.'

'If you could, I'd really appreciate it.'

Joyce made a call. 'If you go up to the first floor, to the east wing, Steve, one of our RNs, will meet you there. But you'll need to sign the visitors' book first,' she told him as she handed him a visitor badge.

Xavier did as he was instructed; he signed in and then made his way to the east wing, where Steve was waiting for him.

He was a big burly man in his early thirties. His hair had a buzz cut and he was heavily tattooed but his uniform was neatly ironed, his shoes were polished and his nails clean. He looked like ex-defence force and Xavier wondered what made him work here. His look was unexpected but he must have chosen to work here and if he was here because he wanted to be, not just for the pay cheque, then Xavier had learned from experience that would make him an excellent nurse. It was a vocation, not just a job.

'Dr O'Donnell?'

'Xavier, please.'

'You want some information on HD?'

Xavier nodded and repeated his reason for the visit.

'We are one of the only care facilities in Australia to have a specialised HD unit. We can accommodate twenty sufferers at a time,' Steve told him as they walked along a corridor. 'Most people are cared for at home initially, until it gets too much for the families, either physically or emotionally. The majority of our HD patients need twenty-four-hour care, which becomes virtually impossible in a home environment.' Steve punched a code into an electronic keypad at the end of the corridor and pushed open the door. 'This is our day room.'

Steve stopped just inside the room and his voice was low and quiet as he explained the situation further to Xavier. 'The majority of our patients are late stage and many have lost the power of speech so you won't be able to talk to them. Many sufferers choose not to get to this stage; some choose to find another way out. Huntington's is hard on the sufferer and on the families. There's no cure. No hope. It's a waiting game; the end is just a matter of time.' Steve paused as Xavier looked around the room.

He saw several wheelchair-bound residents. Some were being fed but many had naso-gastric tubes, obviously no longer able to swallow. The room was large and light with pretty views out to the gardens and the gum trees but Xavier knew these patients would never walk out there and might not even remember what it was like to be mobile.

'You're wanting to know more about the impact on a family rather than the symptoms and progress of the disease, correct?' Steve asked. When Xavier nodded Steve added, 'Give me a minute, would you?'

He left Xavier and went to speak to an elderly woman who was spoon-feeding a younger woman. Xavier watched the interaction.

'Merilyn is happy to talk to you,' Steve said when he returned. 'She can give you her perspective if you like. Why don't you grab a coffee and take her outside?' he suggested. 'She could do with a change of scenery. She spends a lot of time with her daughter.'

Xavier bought sandwiches and coffee from the café on the ground floor and followed Merilyn to a wooden bench.

'You want to know what it's like living with Huntington's?' Merilyn asked as she sat down.

Xavier nodded. 'My partner—' he really had no idea how to describe Brighde and he suspected she'd have a fit if she could hear him but she wasn't there; this was all up to him and he was determined to find out everything he needed today; he didn't plan on coming back '—is pregnant. HD runs in her family and she is understandably concerned about the risk. She nursed her mother through the disease but I have no experience with it whatsoever and I'm trying to get an idea of what she went through. Of what we might be facing in the future.'

'You didn't use pre-implantation testing? That's been an option for years now.'

'We didn't plan the pregnancy,' Xavier admitted.

He could see the look of surprise on Merilyn's face but it was only there briefly before her expression went blank. She obviously had an opinion about their recklessness that she had decided to keep to herself.

'Are you going to test now? Before the baby is born?' she asked.

Xavier was appreciative of the fact that Merilyn had agreed to talk to him and he wanted to be honest even though he had no idea how she might interpret his candidness. 'I want to do the test but my partner wants to terminate. I'm not sure that I agree with her and that's why I'm here—to try to see things from her point of view.'

'Well, I can't speak for her but I can speak on behalf of the families of sufferers. I love my daughter and I would never wish that she hadn't been born but I *do* wish that she hadn't been born with HD. I wish that every day. It is a horrible disease.'

'But you chose to have a family.'

'The disease runs in my husband's family.

Elise is forty-nine now and things were different fifty years ago. The disease was never talked about, never discussed, in his family and it was like that in many families who suffered the same fate. Because of the shortened life expectancy of sufferers, most die somewhere between their forties to sixties; many of us had already had children before we learned that there was a family history. It was brushed under the carpet and not spoken of, certainly never by its correct name, and a lot of sufferers were diagnosed with other afflictions—dementia, alcoholism and the like. Not a lot was known about HD when Norm and I got married—the gene was only identified in 1986—and even less could be done. Testing wasn't available when I had my children and pre-implantation testing wasn't available until Elise was nearly thirty-four. By then my husband had died from the disease. Elise and her sister had watched their father succumb to the disease.' She paused before asking, 'Are you sure you want to hear all this?'

Xavier nodded. 'As long as you don't mind talking about it.'

'My husband became aggressive and mean,' Merilyn continued. 'We had to keep reminding ourselves that this was a result of the disease, that he couldn't control it, but every day was a struggle to keep our family together. Elise was profoundly affected by the changes in her father and she decided early on that she wouldn't have children. She became a kindergarten teacher and those kids became her surrogate children.'

Brighde's choice of career sprang to Xavier's mind. She'd told him she'd never planned to have children, that she got her fill of babies at work. Had she chosen her career because of her family history?

Was he being unfair? Was he putting undue pressure on her? He hoped that if the babies were okay that she would be happy. But maybe she still wouldn't be. How did she really feel? She had told him she would love children of her own providing she hadn't passed on the gene but he had no idea if that was true. Maybe she really didn't want children, no matter what, and was using HD as an excuse. He really wasn't sure of the answers.

'I have two daughters and they both chose to get tested as soon as that was an option. Sometimes I wish they hadn't.'

'Why is that?'

'Carmel tested negative, Elise obviously didn't and that put a terrible strain on their relationship. They'd always been close until then. After the diagnosis, Elise got depression—it's a very common outcome—and that changed her long before her symptoms became apparent. Sometimes I think the diagnosis was the beginning of the end. She had no symptoms yet but everything changed from that day.'

Again, Xavier was able to see the similarities between Merilyn's family and Brighde's. Brighde and her brother had made a pact not to get tested for HD but what effect had Nick's change of mind had on Brighde? Would she be even more worried now, not only about her test results, but how that might affect her relationship with her brother? There were so many things to consider. So much more than just the physical aspects of the disease. He was beginning to understand just how complicated this all was and the stress that Brighde would be under.

'Elise's physical symptoms started about nine years ago but, by then, we had battled with her depression for six years already. Her balance was one of the first things affected. She had been a competitive swimmer but gymnastics might have been a better option to counteract the decline in her balance. At this stage the disease has affected her ability to walk, talk and think. Next to go will be her ability to swallow and she will end up being tube fed. I am seventy-four years old. It's taken forty years of my life and people would say I'm the lucky one, that I don't have the disease. But I've lived it twice over.'

Merilyn had nursed her husband and now her daughter. Xavier knew she'd been beaten down by the disease; he could hear it in her voice and see it in her face. Listening to Merilyn, he could hear how difficult her life had been. Not only had her husband and daughter been afflicted but even Merilyn's memories of them were being replaced by more recent, devastating memories. Her story was heartbreaking and he suspected it was very similar to Brighde's story.

He was so relieved that he hadn't asked Brighde to accompany him today—he hadn't really had any idea how emotional this would be—but, talking to Merilyn, he felt like he could be talking to a future Brighde. Her mother had died at forty-nine, the same age as Merilyn's daughter was now. That surely would have brought Brighde's memories to the fore and he was glad he hadn't subjected her to that.

He knew Brighde had watched her mother suffer, had nursed her through the early stages of the disease and was now facing the possibility of doing it all over again with her own child. *Their* child. And, potentially, both babies could be affected. Xavier knew he couldn't put her through that. It wasn't only the person with the faulty gene who suffered; it was the entire family.

'Do you have any words of advice for me?' he asked.

Merilyn shook her head. 'I'm not going to tell you what is right or wrong. I'm not going to give you any advice except to say that everyone has their choice to make and don't judge someone for what they choose to do or not to do. Not before you've walked a mile in their shoes.'

Xavier nodded and stood up. 'Thank you for talking to me; I really appreciate it.' And now he needed to talk to Brighde.

Sarah answered his knock on the door.

'Hi. Is Brighde home?'

'She's just gone down to the shops. Are you okay? You don't look well.'

He felt awful. Merilyn's insight had been an eye-opener for him. He'd done his research and thought he had been prepared for the visual side but he hadn't been prepared for the emotional side. Listening to Merilyn had been confronting. An awakening. An emotional punch in the face—there had been so many parallels between Brighde's life and Merilyn's. He wasn't surprised to hear he looked terrible. It had been a lot to absorb. 'I've just been to see some HD patients.'

'Oh.' Sarah stepped aside, holding the door open. 'I think you'd better come in. Brighde won't be long. Can I get you something to drink? You look like you could use a whisky.'

He would love a drink to take the edge off the pain he was feeling but he knew that was nothing compared to what Brighde had been through. 'No. Thank you, but I need to keep a clear head.'

'So, how did it go?' Sarah asked as he followed her inside. 'It's pretty confronting, isn't it?'

Xavier nodded. 'It was one of the worst things I've ever experienced and, considering I've been a doctor for ten years, that's quite a statement.'

'So you see why Brighde feels the way she does?'

'Yes, I can.'

'What are you going to do?'

'I'm going to speak to her again about having an amnio.'

If he wanted her to have the test he knew he had to agree with her conditions. If he didn't she could terminate the pregnancy without his consent *and* without getting tested. The amniocentesis was the only chance he had of convincing her to have the babies; therefore he had no choice but to agree to her decision regarding the pregnancy if the babies had a positive score on their CAG repeats. He knew that was the only way.

'If she agrees to the amnio you can't ask her to go through with the pregnancy if the test comes back positive. It would destroy her,' Sarah said. 'No matter what happens, she's already a victim of the disease. She lost her mother and lost contact with her father because of it. She's scared. You need to understand and respect that.'

Brighde held all the cards. He knew that. She'd lost both her parents because of the disease and he couldn't ask her to go through it again with her own child. She might not have the symptoms but if she had passed on the mutated gene she wouldn't escape the suffering or the guilt and he couldn't ask her to spend half a lifetime with her child only to then watch that life disappear in a terrible fashion. But he also couldn't agree to take a life now without knowing the future. If Brighde would agree to an amniocentesis, he would agree with her subsequent decision.

'I do. I get it. She's agreed to having an amnio on certain conditions. Having seen what I did today, I'm prepared to agree to her terms,' he said as they heard the sound of Brighde's key unlocking the front door.

Brighde was surprised to see Xavier sitting in her kitchen. She didn't think they'd made plans but she couldn't be one hundred per cent sure. She'd been extremely forgetful of late. She didn't think it was pregnancy brain, more likely a symptom of everything that was on her mind. There was no room for the little day-to-day things when her head was so full of big decisions that needed to be made.

'Hi. Sorry, have I forgotten something?'

'No,' he said as he stood up.

He looked uncomfortable. Uncertain. It was the first time she could remember seeing him ill at ease.

'Is something wrong?' she asked. He didn't look his usual robust self. He was still gorgeous—she doubted he could look anything else—but he looked exhausted, drained.

'You were right,' was all he said.

'About what?'

'Huntington's Disease and what it does.'

'You went to the care facility?'

He nodded.

'Are you okay?'

'Not really,' he admitted as they sat at the kitchen table. 'But this isn't about me. I spoke to a woman there. A mother. She was visiting her daughter. She'd nursed her husband and then her daughter. She was strong but you could tell it has destroyed her. You were right; I didn't understand what it was like. I'm not sure I really do, even now, but it's a lot clearer. The pain, the helplessness. I'm sorry I've made this difficult for you.' He picked up her hand. 'If you will have the amnio I will be guided by you when we get the results. It's all up to you.'

'Are you saying that if the result is positive you won't fight a termination?'

Xavier nodded. 'That's what I'm saying. But I need to ask: if the tests are negative what are your plans then? Would a negative test result change your mind about having a family of your own? Would you have the babies?'

'Of course.'

'You're happy about the pregnancy?'

'Not completely,' she admitted. 'Not yet. I never thought I would have children—you know I never planned to—but *if* the test is negative, if everything is okay, then yes, I will be happy. But I can't allow myself to think like that yet. I'm scared I might still be disappointed, that it will all come crashing down and that would be devastating.'

'There's something else,' he said. Brighde expected him to look pleased that she would be prepared to give him the children he was so desperate for but there was still a crease of concern running between his brows. 'Have you thought about what would happen if only one twin tested negative? What would you do then?'

Brighde frowned. It was a possibility, given that they suspected the babies were non-identical, but, once again, it was another thing she hadn't thought through. 'I'm not sure. Would selective reduction be an option, do you think?' She knew it was possible to abort one twin but she didn't know the details.

'Yes. But the further along the pregnancy is, the more difficult that becomes. And there's also the risk of losing both. The longer you wait, the harder it is.'

'Even if Julie can do the amnio this week it will take a couple of weeks to get the results back. I'll be twenty weeks by then.' Her voice was laced with worry; she could hear it.

'That's okay, but it's something you need to think about over the next fortnight. I know you'd rather not have to deal with it but, if it comes to that, time will be of the essence. It's better to think about that scenario now so you're prepared.'

Brighde could see Xavier's point. She had to get all her facts straight. She needed to get her ducks in a row and then she'd be able to make informed decisions. That *had* to be better than making decisions based on guesswork.

She would make an appointment with Julie for an amniocentesis.

'Are you okay?' he asked as she sat on the edge of the examination bed. She'd asked him to accompany her this time. He was calm, unflappable and knew what to expect. She wouldn't have to explain anything to him or worry about him coping with the procedure. Sarah would have accompanied her but having Xavier there was the right thing to do. And she wanted him there.

She had never gotten over her father leaving her and Nick to cope with their mother's disease on their own and she was terrified of having to face more tragedy without support. 'I'm scared.'

It felt as if she was permanently afraid of late. This pregnancy was very real to her now. Her body was changing: her boobs were bigger, her stomach a little rounder. Her morning sickness had almost resolved and this morning she'd felt flutterings in her stomach that she knew was the babies moving. She would have loved to share that information with Xavier but she still didn't want to invest too much emotion into this pregnancy. It would destroy her if she got too attached, only to find out she had to terminate.

Her whole attitude had changed and now she was praying that her babies would be okay. She couldn't imagine the alternative. Not any more.

Xavier held her hand. 'I'm right here. You don't have to do this alone,' he said as Julie came into the room.

'Good morning. How are you feeling, Brighde?'

'I'm really nervous,' she admitted. 'And apprehensive.'

'About the test itself or the result?'

'Both.'

'The amnio may be a little uncomfortable—'

Brighde shook her head and interrupted. 'It's not the discomfort that's bothering me. It's the risk.'

'There's a small risk of miscarriage associated with amniocentesis,' Julie told her, 'The risk decreases after fifteen weeks' gestation so that's good news for you at eighteen weeks. There's no clear reason as to the cause of miscarriage; it may be due to infection or trauma to the amniotic sac. Here in Victoria it's about one in two hundred into the second trimester and my statistics are a bit better than that. In theory, about one in twenty women miscarry before twelve weeks but you do already have an increased risk because of a twin pregnancy. But, with regard to the amnio, because your twins are fraternal I need to take two separate samples. So the risk is the same but the likelihood of a miscarriage is slightly higher because you are having two needle aspirations. That's the facts. I'm not sure if that will help to put your mind at ease but you do need to know the risks before we go ahead. Do you still want to do this?'

Brighde knew she didn't really have a choice. As frightened as she was of having the procedure, she was more afraid of passing on the gene. This was the only way to know for sure. She nodded and squeezed Xavier's hand a little more tightly.

'I'll do the amnio under ultrasound guidance,' Julie said as she switched on the machine, 'so let's have a look at your babies.'

Brighde lifted her shirt and turned her eyes to the screen as Julie moved the transducer head over her abdomen.

'There's Twin A,' Julie said as the image of one tiny baby came onto the screen.

'He's a little footballer. Look at him kicking,' Xavier said. If Brighde hadn't been so nervous she would have smiled at the note of pride in his voice.

'Girls can play football too,' she said. With the way the baby was positioned she couldn't see anything to suggest the sex and she knew Xavier was just using a figure of speech but she was convinced both babies were girls.

Julie paused the image and clicked buttons, measuring the foetus. 'Fourteen centimetres. Just what we hope for at this stage.' She printed a picture and then moved the machine onto Twin B.

'She's sucking her thumb!' Brighde exclaimed.

'Do you want me to take the measurements for foetal anomalies?' Julie asked as she measured Twin B's length.

'Can you do the amnio first?' Brighde asked. 'I want to get that over and done with.' She really was nervous about the test and wanted it out of the way as soon as possible.

'Of course,' Julie replied. 'Now, the results are about ninety-nine per cent accurate. Do either of you have any questions before I begin?'

Xavier and Brighde both shook their heads.

'I'll just put a bit of local anaesthetic on your tummy, Brighde, and call the technician to monitor the ultrasound.'

Julie gave the anaesthetic time to work but when she pulled out the long, thin biopsy needle Brighde turned her head. She didn't want to watch the procedure. She held on tight to Xavier's hand and kept her eyes focused on his gorgeous face. He smiled at her and kissed her. The kiss was unexpected and Brighde's heartbeat picked up its pace. If his intention was to distract her it was working.

Xavier had been so gentle and considerate recently. He was thoughtful and gorgeous and just what she'd imagined she'd look for in a boyfriend if she'd ever let herself have one. But even though they were spending time together she hadn't slept with him again. She was trying hard to keep some distance between them. She didn't want things to become messy or awkward so, no matter how much she longed to share physical intimacy, she knew she couldn't risk it. Her heart was conflicted enough with the idea of a pregnancy; she couldn't afford to throw an intimate relationship with Xavier into the mix. She would love to be able to say he was her partner or boyfriend but that would be taking things further than she could handle at the moment.

'Do you want to know the sex of the babies?' Julie asked. 'The test will be definitive on that too.'

'I'm not sure,' Brighde replied. Even though she felt they were girls she hadn't actually thought about finding out. She hadn't dared to think too far ahead.

'Do you want to know what I think?' Xavier said.

'What?'

'I think we're having a pigeon pair. A boy and a girl.'

He sounded so certain that Brighde wondered if he'd glimpsed something on the ultrasound that she'd missed. 'Did you see something?'

'No—' he grinned and Brighde's heart did a little flip in her chest '—did you?'

She shook her head.

'What do you think they are?'

'Two girls.'

'Why?'

'I have no idea.'

'Shall we have a bet on it?'

'I am *not* betting on the sex of our children.'

'Why not?'

'I don't trust you. I think you saw something.'

'Cross my heart. Shall we find out officially?'

'No.' She didn't want to know for sure until they had the results and she'd made a decision about what would happen next. She felt knowing the babies' sex might strengthen the attachment she was beginning to feel and that would only make things more difficult if the results came back positive. She couldn't afford to get too attached. Just in case.

'Okay, I'm all done,' Julie said.

'Thank you,' Brighde said to Xavier.

'What for?'

'For distracting me.'

'Did it work?'

'Yep.'

'All right, next question,' Julie said. 'The anomaly scan?'

'I'm not sure,' Brighde said as she looked at Xavier. This test would check for other more common anomalies like Down Syndrome. Brighde didn't think she would terminate a pregnancy in that case but, like many other things, she and Xavier hadn't actually discussed this.

'It's not just for Down syndrome,' Julie said when Brighde posed the question. 'There are a whole host of things we look for. You know that. I will check the heart, kidneys, spine, palate and stomach plus take some further measurements of the head, abdomen and thigh and also check your placenta.'

Xavier was nodding. Of course he'd want the tests done. He liked to be prepared.

'Okay,' Brighde agreed.

It took another hour to scan both babies, by

which time Brighde thought her bladder would burst, but Julie hadn't finished with her yet.

'Miscarriage will usually occur in the first seventy-two hours after testing so I recommend that you take it easy for the next few days,' she said as she helped Brighde to sit up. 'You don't need bed rest but you have got time off work, right?'

Brighde nodded. 'Three days.'

'Good. Tell me if I'm singing to the choir, won't you, but I know from when I was pregnant myself that being on the other side of the fence is a very different experience. So much of your medical knowledge seems to disappear into the ether when it's your own children. So, don't forget about what can be perfectly normal happenings after an amnio. Things like mild, period-like cramping abdominal pains with some light spotting. You can take paracetamol to help ease the pain. The results will take a couple of weeks. I'll call you to schedule an appointment when the results are back.'

'You know,' Xavier said once Julie had left

the room, 'during the amnio you said "our children". That's the first time you've said that.'

Brighde frowned. 'No, it isn't.'

'Yes, it is. You've said "my children" and "your children" but never "our children". Does that mean you've been thinking that we might be able to make a go of this? That maybe we could have a future. Not just co-parenting but the two of us, together.'

'What do you mean? Together?'

'I think we should get married.'

'What? Why on earth would you want to get married?'

'It's not about getting married. It's about showing you my commitment. To you and the babies. Showing you that, whatever happens, you can rely on me. That I'll be there to support you.'

'Marriage is no guarantee of that. Trust me, I know. And I'm still no closer to knowing what I'm going to do yet, Xavier. I'm not making any more decisions until we get the results of the amnio back. I'm not doing anything until I know my children's future.'

'Our children.'

'Our children.' She did like the sound of that phrase and she couldn't disagree—he'd been very considerate and supportive of her so far—but marriage was no guarantee of commitment. She'd seen evidence of that first-hand with her own parents.

'Would you think about it at least?' he asked. 'If not from your point of view, how about from the babies'? Surely having parents who are married gives them that stability and surely that is best for them?'

She couldn't help but wonder if his suggestion was only tied in to his desire to be a father. Was it his way of making sure she couldn't leave him out?

'Don't be ridiculous. The babies won't know and won't care if we're married. Having two parents who love each other is best for children. Having parents who are going to live a long, healthy, happy life is best for the children.

As a matter of fact, having a parent who would not choose an early death sentence for a child is best for the child. Marriage isn't the answer.'

'But it's my promise. My way of showing you that I will be there for you and our children,' he argued.

'You can't promise that. And I've told you, I'm not going to inflict this disease on my children—that's why we're doing these tests—and if they have escaped the mutation there is still no reason to get married. Any promises you made would only be false ones if there's no relationship between us to begin with.' Xavier wasn't in love with her. How could she trust him to stick around and support her if they started out with nothing substantial between them in the first place? 'I don't *want* to get married.'

'Why not?'

'Because relationships don't last. Marriages don't last. Not even love is enough to get people through the tough times and there is no way I can trust a marriage that is based on a misguided sense of duty to survive.'

'It's more than duty,' he said. 'We have plenty of chemistry. That's something. I know marriages that have started with less.'

'Chemistry isn't enough to get us past our first wedding anniversary, let alone all the obstacles we could be facing. Neither of us should expect everlasting married happiness, given what we've seen. Your girlfriend cheated on you and my father walked out on us.'

'We are not those people. What they did doesn't define us.'

But Brighde had spent too many years avoiding relationships to change her mind that easily now. There was a reason she didn't date. She didn't want to fall in love. To fall in love was to risk everything.

And while knowing she wasn't going to develop HD had unlocked an alternative door to her future, she still couldn't afford to think about marriage yet—no matter how much she wanted to. She had to wait for the results of the amniocentesis now before she could think ahead and, regardless of those results, she couldn't have it all. Xavier wasn't offering his love and she refused to be married to someone out of an obligation.

She shook her head. 'I can't marry you.'

'I don't know what to do.'

Xavier sat at his sister's kitchen table, nursing a whisky. Mary's husband was putting the kids to bed and Xavier was picking Mary's brains. Her suggestion to get Brighde out of Melbourne and into a fresh environment had prompted their trip to Daylesford and he hoped she'd have more good advice this time. 'I know Brighde's stressed about the amnio results but she's barely speaking to me.'

'You can't blame her for being stressed. From what you've told me, it's a terrible disease and she must be worried sick that one or both of the twins might have it. She must be terrified and I can't imagine that she's got the energy to worry about you too. I know what it's like. Sometimes there's a limit to what you can focus on. Give her time.'

'But we need to think about the future.'

'That's a bit difficult at the moment. The future might change in the blink of an eye, depending on the amnio results. If you want my advice, I'm telling you to just be patient. I know it's not always your forte. I know you don't like to wait, but there's nothing you can do about the test results and I don't think you can expect Brighde to move forwards until she has those.'

'I promised her that if the test results came back positive I wouldn't oppose a termination, but I don't think I can give the babies up.' Xavier could see Brighde's point of view about a termination but he still couldn't imagine ending the life of a child—his child. But he was fast running out of ideas of ways to get around her concerns.

'So what are your options?'

'I don't really have any. It's all up to Brighde.'

'As long as she knows you're there for her. That's what she needs at the moment.'

'I'm not sure that she wants that either. I asked her to marry me. She said no.'

'Why?'

'Why what? Why did I ask her to marry me or why did she say no?'

'Both, I guess.'

'I wanted her to know she has my support and I thought getting married would show her I meant to stick around. I thought she'd appreciate it after her father walked out on them when she was very young. That's really messed her up and I thought I was doing the right thing.'

'Her parents were married, weren't they?'

'Yes.'

'And her father still left. In Brighde's mind, marriage probably isn't the promise you think it is.'

'But marriage makes sense.'

'Getting married only makes sense if you love each other. Do you love her?'

Did he?

'She's going to be the mother of my children,' he replied, not sure he was ready to give an answer. He thought he'd been in love with his ex-girlfriend but that was nothing compared to the way he felt about Brighde. Brighde was different—she lit up his life and he couldn't picture his future without her in it. He thought he could be falling in love with her but she kept pushing him away.

'That's not necessarily love. Would you marry her if she wasn't pregnant? I know you love the idea of settling down, getting married, having a family of your own, but there are lots of ways to do that. Marriage may not be your only future. Brighde can still be in your future without marriage. There's nothing wrong with choosing to co-parent. Plenty of people opt for that and do it successfully. Marriage isn't for everyone.'

'But it is for me.'

'I know that but maybe it's not for Brighde. Give her some space. Don't crowd her but don't desert her either.'

'How do I do both?'

'You're a smart man. You'll figure it out. She *will* need you. She might not need a husband but she will need your support, no matter what happens. And if everything goes well she will need a father for her children—your children. Don't muck this up. Give her what she needs.'

She needed him.

No, she didn't.

But she did need someone to love her. And that someone was him.

He would tell her how he felt. He would give this one last shot. All or nothing, he decided. Go hard or go home.

Brighde opened her eyes and checked her alarm. Something had woken her but it was still half an hour before she needed to get up. She had taken three days off after the amniocentesis but she was due back at work today.

As she lay in bed she felt a fluttering in her belly. Maybe the babies had woken her. She smiled and put her hand on her stomach. She was scared to admit it but she had bonded with her babies and with every breath she took she hoped that they would be all right. That maybe they would all get through this. But she knew she wouldn't relax until the test results came back. There was still too much at stake.

She rolled onto her side. She would stay in bed for a little longer; there was no hurry to get up. She would lie still and see if she could feel any more tiny movements. She liked to think of the twins communicating with each other as they wriggled and kicked.

She waited until her alarm rang before getting out of bed but she had only taken four steps into the hallway when she felt a sharp pain in her side. That wasn't a fluttering; it was a strong cramp. She clutched her side and put her other hand on the wall to steady herself as she took a deep breath and waited for the cramp to pass. It subsided but, before she could move, she felt something warm running down the inside of her thigh. She put her hand between her legs. It came out red.

CHAPTER NINE

'SARAH!'

Brighde's voice echoed in the hallway, bouncing off the floorboards and the walls, and Sarah burst out of her room, spurred on by Brighde's cries. She took one look at Brighde, who was leaning against the hallway wall, her hand and legs smeared with blood.

Sarah's eyes were wide. 'We need to get you to the hospital.'

Brighde nodded mutely. Her heart was racing and her knees shook. She didn't want to lose her babies.

Sarah grabbed a cardigan and wrapped it around Brighde's shoulders. She yanked a towel from the linen cupboard, picked up her keys and both of their phones from the hall table and bundled Brighde into her car. 'Is Xavier's number in your phone?' she asked as she put her seat belt on.

Brighde nodded again and Sarah called the number. She heard her leave a message.

'Xavier, Brighde is bleeding. I'm taking her to Parkville.'

Sarah ended the call and pulled the car into the traffic as Brighde sobbed quietly in her seat. She had her hands resting on her stomach, willing these babies to stay put. These babies she'd never dreamed she would have were now the most important things in her life. She couldn't bear to lose them.

Sarah drove her car into the turning circle at the front entrance to the hospital and Xavier was the first thing Brighde noticed. He was pacing up and down the driveway, an empty wheelchair abandoned to one side. The moment he saw Sarah's car he was by the door, opening it almost before Sarah had stopped completely. He scooped Brighde into his arms and carried her to the wheelchair.

'I'll take her upstairs,' he said over his shoulder to Sarah.

He pushed Brighde into the foyer; avoiding the emergency department, he wheeled her to the lifts. 'I've called Julie. She'll meet us in Maternity,' he told Brighde as they waited. He didn't tell her everything would be okay. She knew he couldn't but she longed to hear those words anyway.

He wheeled her into an exam room and lifted her onto the bed.

She curled herself into a ball and faced the wall. She couldn't bear to look at him.

She wondered if it was something she'd done. Maybe she'd strained something? But she couldn't imagine how; she'd barely done anything for the past three days but that didn't stop her from worrying. From feeling guilty. She'd never forgive herself if she had caused this and she couldn't bear to look at Xavier. She couldn't bear to see any recrimination in his dark eyes.

She didn't need anyone else questioning her actions or wondering what had gone wrong.

Because in her heart she knew that something was wrong. Something was *very* wrong.

There was way too much blood.

She heard the door open, heard Xavier greeting Julie.

She turned her head as she listened to Xavier telling Julie the little he knew.

Someone had to help her. Someone had to do something.

'I think I might be losing the babies,' she said as she burst into another flood of tears.

Xavier was by her side. He pulled a chair closer to the bed as he grabbed some tissues from the dispenser on the wall and pressed them into her hand. He sat beside her and stroked the hair back from her face.

'When did the bleeding start?' Julie asked as she snapped on a pair of surgical gloves.

'Maybe an hour ago,' Brighde told her. She wasn't really sure what the time was. Everything was a blur since she'd started to bleed.

'Are you in pain?' Julie asked as she attached

monitors to Brighde to record her blood pressure, heart rate and oxygen saturation.

She was scared and anxious and felt as though her heart was breaking but she knew that wasn't what Julie was asking. 'No.' She'd only had the one cramp and, while it had been painful, it didn't come close to the pain in her heart.

Maybe it was nothing. Maybe it was just a bit of spotting. But in her heart she knew that wasn't the case.

Something had gone wrong. She could feel it.

'Any temperature?'

'I don't think so,' Brighde replied as Julie picked up the thermometer and popped it into her ear.

'That's normal,' she said as the thermometer beeped. 'Let's have a look, shall we?'

Brighde had come to hospital in the old T-shirt she'd worn to bed. She had Sarah's cardigan wrapped around her and a towel between her thighs. Her underwear was soaked in blood. Julie lifted Brighde's shirt and removed the towel. Brighde saw the look that Julie and Xavier exchanged as they examined the towel.

It was stained with dark red blood.

'I'll need to do a scan,' Julie said. 'That will show us what's going on.'

Brighde waited in silence while Julie got the machine ready and ran it over her abdomen. She couldn't speak. She couldn't think straight. All she wanted was to hear that her babies were fine.

Julie kept the screen turned away from Brighde and she didn't think she could bear the suspense. 'What can you see?'

'Twin B is fine. I can see a heartbeat and the rate is perfectly normal,' Julie said, keeping her eyes on the monitor.

'And Twin A? What about Twin A?' Brighde could hear a trace of hysteria creeping into her voice as Xavier picked up her hand and held it. Tight.

Julie was shaking her head. 'I'm sorry, Brighde; there's only one heartbeat.'

'No!'

'Let me see.'

'Brighde—'

She heard the note of warning in Xavier's voice but she knew she wouldn't believe it until she'd seen it with her own eyes.

She turned to face him. His eyes were brimming with unshed tears. Shiny and bright.

'I need to see.'

He nodded slowly as Julie turned the screen to face her and moved the ultrasound head around, capturing the picture.

Two sacs, two tiny babies, but only one heartbeat.

Tears streamed down Brighde's cheeks. The front of her T-shirt was soaking wet. 'No! Why? What happened?'

'Often we don't know why these things happen,' Julie said as she lifted the transducer head from Brighde's stomach and the image disappeared.

Brighde lifted one hand, reaching for the screen, trying to bring her babies back. 'But they were both fine three days ago.'

'You had a viable pregnancy three days ago, but that's all we know.'

'Was it the amnio?'

'It could have been but I think it's more likely to be unrelated. The amniotic sacs are both intact and you don't have a temperature so I don't think there's an infection but I'll take a blood sample and we'll check that. As you know, there is a much higher rate of miscarriage with twin pregnancies. I'm sorry.'

'What happens now?' Brighde felt like she should know but her brain seemed to have completely shut down. Nothing made sense.

'I'm going to admit you. I want you to have bed rest for a few days.'

'I have to stay here?'

'I think it's the best place for you. We can keep an eye on you here. We need to make sure the bleeding stops and I need to monitor the other twin.'

'You think I might lose the other baby?'

'I couldn't say for certain. The twins were dizygotic and dichorionic—two sacs and two placentas—and being non-identical reduces the risk of both miscarrying. Plus your general health is good. These things are all in your favour, which lessens the likelihood of a second miscarriage, but I can't make any promises. So, for now we wait. There's nothing you can do. I'll take some blood and you rest and I'll see if I can get the amnio results through a little faster.'

'Once the bleeding has stopped, what then?' Brighde asked as Julie took a blood sample. 'What happens to the babies?'

'If you don't have any cramping and the blood tests are normal, so no sign of infection, then once the bleeding stops I will discharge you. We shouldn't need to do anything more except closely monitor Twin B.'

'And the other baby? What happens to the other baby?'

'The sac is intact. Both babies can stay in there for as long as possible. Given the chorionicity, your gestational age and your health, letting your pregnancy continue is low-risk. I don't want to do any unnecessary procedures.'

'Can you tell me if Twin A was a boy or a girl? I'd like to know.' She didn't ask Xavier. She had to know now.

'A boy.'

Brighde closed her eyes. She'd lost their son.

She opened her eyes. 'And the other one?'

'A girl.'

Xavier had been right. She turned to look at him. He had tears in his eyes but he hadn't said a word.

Did he blame her? Did he think this was her fault? She knew how much he wanted these babies; he'd made that perfectly clear on many occasions. Would he think this was her fault?

She didn't dare ask what he was thinking; she was too scared of the answer.

'We'll get you cleaned up and admitted,' Julie said, interrupting her thoughts. 'I'll be back to see you later.'

Brighde was in a private room, attached to a drip and various other electrodes, lying in bed while Xavier hovered. There was nothing for him to do; there was nothing he *could* do and his presence was irritating her. She still didn't want to look at him, still couldn't bear it. She didn't want to see her loss and despair reflected back at her from the depths of his eyes. She was feeling terrible enough already.

'Don't you have patients to see?' she asked.

'I've rescheduled or postponed them,' he replied. 'I can stay as long as you need me.'

'I don't need you. I think you should go.'

'What? Why?' She could see the confusion in his eyes. But that was better than accusations.

'Don't you see? I shouldn't even *be* pregnant. I've just lost one baby and I might lose the other one too. I shouldn't *be* in this position and I wouldn't be if it wasn't for you. Every time I look at you I'm reminded of what I've lost or might still lose. I don't want to see you. I just want to be alone.'

'Brighde, you don't have to be alone. I'm here for you.' He'd stopped pacing and was standing by her bed, a worried expression on his gorgeous face. He reached out one hand towards her but when she folded her arms across her chest, blocking him out, his hand dropped to his side. 'I'm hurting too, Brighde.'

'It's not the same. You've never lost anyone.'

'This baby was ours. Yours and mine. I've lost just as much as you have. Don't shut me out. I want this baby more than anything.'

Was that part of the problem? She knew it was. Xavier wanted the baby but he wasn't talking about wanting her any more. Had his suggestion of marriage been his way of making sure he was in his children's lives? Making sure she couldn't cut him out? She had never intended to do that but, right now, she just didn't want to see him. She needed some space. 'I don't want you here,' she said bluntly and she could see she'd hurt him but she was hurting more.

He stood, watching her silently, for what seemed like hours before, eventually, he nodded. 'I will go now but I'm not walking out of your life. You can keep sending me away but

I'll keep coming back. I can be just as stubborn as you.'

Brighde closed her eyes and turned her head away, waiting until she heard him leave, until she heard the door close.

She was better off alone.

That was what she'd always thought but meeting Xavier had made her believe, just for a short while, that maybe she could have a happily ever after. But it seemed she'd been wrong.

This was all his fault. If she'd never met him she wouldn't be pregnant. If she'd never met him she wouldn't be grieving for a child she'd never expected to have.

How could it hurt so much?

She just wanted to be loved. For her life to have a happy ending. But that was a foolish dream. Everything was unravelling. Everything was out of her control. She never should have let her guard down.

She'd always believed nothing good would ever come of letting someone into her life, into her heart. Well, now she had the proof.

If she'd had any tears left to cry she knew they would be falling. She didn't think her heart could take any more.

CHAPTER TEN

XAVIER LEFT THE room but he wasn't about to leave the hospital. He had nowhere else to go. He'd cancelled his lists so unless someone went into labour he had nowhere to go *and* nothing to do. He didn't think he could face delivering someone else's baby today. His heart was bruised, aching.

He'd lost his child. His son.

Brighde had said he'd never lost anyone before but that wasn't true. He'd lost once before. He remembered when he'd found out that his ex was expecting another man's child, that she wasn't pregnant with his baby. He remembered the day she'd taken that dream from him. He'd thought he could never feel worse than he had that day but to physically lose his own child, his own flesh and blood, was devastating. Heart-breaking.

These babies were real to him and he couldn't bear to think about potentially losing them both or not being allowed to have anything to do with the surviving twin. His daughter. If she made it.

He had to convince Brighde to let him back into her life. He wasn't prepared to lose another child or his chance of fatherhood.

He needed a plan. Another one. And this time it would have to be the perfect plan. Flawless. Because he was in love with a woman who couldn't bear to look at him.

He hadn't had a chance to tell her that he loved her. Or maybe he just hadn't taken the chance. He'd been caught up with other priorities. Had his ex been right? Had he, once again, put too many other things before the important people in his life? Had he not given Brighde the priority she deserved?

He'd have to make things right. He had to let her know how he felt.

He gave her as much time as he could. He

tried catching up on paperwork but found he couldn't concentrate. He tried catching up on journal articles—that was even worse—so eventually he gave up and returned to Brighde's room. She'd have to see him. There were some things that couldn't wait.

He was several rooms away from hers when he saw a couple knock on her door and enter. He couldn't see their faces but the woman was petite and dark and the man was tall and slim with hair the colour of Brighde's with the same thick wave. Was that her brother and sister-in-law? He hesitated. There were some things that couldn't wait but there were also some things that could only be said in private and this was certainly not a discussion he wanted to share with Brighde's brother on their first meeting.

He pulled a chair along the corridor and positioned it outside her room. He'd wait.

He sank into the chair. The adrenalin that had been pumping through him at the thought of declaring his feelings continued to surge through his body but, with no release, the energy it had created left him feeling exhausted. He stretched his legs out and leant back against the wall.

He could hear voices, snippets of conversation, coming from Brighde's room. He didn't mean to eavesdrop but he didn't have the energy to stand and walk away.

He was done walking away.

'You're pregnant?'

A female voice. The sister-in-law?

'Why didn't you tell us?'

Brighde's brother.

Xavier strained to hear her reply. He was interested—very interested—in the answer. He hadn't realised she'd kept her pregnancy a secret. Had she kept *him* a secret?

'Lots of reasons. But mostly because I didn't know what I was going to do about the pregnancy. I didn't know if I would go through with it. I didn't know if I *could.* I was worried about telling you—especially when Immy is pregnant too. I was worried about HD and how you would react if I chose *not* to be pregnant. This wasn't planned. Not at all.'

'What are you going to do?'

'I still don't know. I'm waiting on test results.'

'And the father? Who is he?'

'No one important.'

Pain pierced Xavier's chest. A pain so sharp it made him catch his breath. Was that really how she felt about him? He was imagining a life with her and yet she could dismiss him so easily? Her words cut him to the core. Surely she didn't mean them?

'Does he know about the baby?'

'He knows.'

'And what does he think?'

'That doesn't matter. This was all a mistake. A big mistake.'

Xavier had heard enough. He summoned his energy and stood and walked away. He would retreat but he would return.

His problems were multiplying. He was in love with a woman who wanted nothing to do with him. That presented a challenge but he wasn't defeated. Not yet.

* * *

It had been forty-eight hours since their loss and Brighde was still refusing to see him. Sarah had given him some brief reports but nothing she said eased his concerns. Brighde was barely talking to Sarah either and Sarah suspected she wasn't eating properly. Xavier was concerned she was in real danger of sinking into a depressed state of mind.

He had snuck in late at night to watch her sleeping. She'd been curled into a tight little ball, elbows flexed, hands tucked under her chin. A defensive position. She hadn't looked relaxed even though she was asleep and his heart ached and his arms longed to hold her.

He had finished his morning visits and was hovering near Brighde's room, hoping to catch Julie as she finished her rounds. He saw her walking towards him, a frown between her eyebrows.

'What's going on?' she asked him as she approached.

'What do you mean?'

'I've just seen Brighde to give her the results of her second blood test.'

'Her *second* test?' His heart hammered in his chest. What was wrong now?

'Yes. I asked if she wanted to wait for you. She implied you weren't here.'

'I'm here. I've barely left the hospital for the past few days. What did the blood work show?'

'You know I can't give you Brighde's results,' Julie said as she shook her head. 'You'll have to ask her.'

He hated the rules. The fact that Brighde was the only one with a say. That the father had no rights. 'She's not talking to me,' he admitted. 'She doesn't want me anywhere near her and, from what I hear, she's not doing too well. I'm worried about her but she's not telling me anything.'

Julie considered him carefully before she spoke and he could almost see the wheels turning in her mind. 'Can I ask your professional opinion about one of my patients?'

'Sure.'

'She's a first-time mum who has just lost a baby, a twin. All her blood work has come back clear, no sign of infection, and she's generally healthy.'

'No infection, you said?'

'That's right. I think the miscarriage was probably related to the twin pregnancy. Maybe there was something wrong with the baby but everything seems okay now and she's recovering well, physically, from the loss and I could discharge her but I'm worried about her mental health. We are still waiting on some other test results so I'm considering keeping her here for a couple more days until those results come back. It's not really necessary but I'd feel better if I could keep a close eye on her. What would you do if she was your patient?'

'I'd definitely keep her in.'

'I thought so. Right. Thanks.'

Imogen had been in several times over the past four days, bringing with her pictures of wedding dresses, wedding cakes and bouquets. Brighde knew she was trying to distract her but she wasn't able to get enthused about anything at the moment. Her concentration was shot and she just wasn't interested in what was going on in other people's lives. It was very unlike her but she couldn't shake herself out of the despondency that had settled over her. She wasn't sleeping or eating properly either, which she knew was only making things worse, but her appetite had deserted her along with her sense of humour.

Now it seemed it was Sarah's turn to try to jolly her out of her slump. Although she'd chosen a strange topic to try to cheer Brighde up.

'So, have you seen Xavier?' Sarah asked as she rearranged a bunch of flowers on the bedside table, pulling out a few sad, droopy stems in an effort to revitalise the display.

Brighde wished she could do the same to her. Pull out the sad pieces of her heart and plump it up with some fresh water. She wished it was that easy to bring her back to life.

'No.' She still wasn't ready to see him. To see the sadness in his eyes. She didn't have the energy to deal with his grief as well as her own.

'You can't put it off for ever. He is still going to be the father of your child.'

'I know.' But there was still a possibility that she could lose this baby too and then there would be no need to see Xavier. There would be no need to have anything to do with him. She was convinced he was only interested in their child and where did that leave her? 'But I could lose this one too. There's no point in speaking to him until I know for certain what's going on. I haven't even got the amnio results back yet.' The lack of information was hanging over her head like a big black cloud.

'You are nineteen weeks pregnant. This baby looks perfectly happy; there's no reason to think anything untoward will happen. If everything comes back clear, which I'm sure it will, then I think you two need to have a serious conversation.'

'About what?'

'Life, the universe and everything in between. You are going to have to find a way to work things out. You'll be tied together for ever through this baby. If you wanted to you might even get to live happily ever after.'

'I don't think so,' Brighde said with a shake of her head. 'He doesn't love me.'

'Has he told you that?'

'He hasn't told me he does. Everything he's done has been about the baby,' she replied just as her OB/GYN entered the room.

'Good morning, Brighde,' Julie said as she breezed in. Everyone's spirits seemed high today, Brighde thought. Everyone, that was, except for her.

'Please, can I wait just a bit for another ultrasound?' Brighde asked, assuming that Julie was planning another scan. She'd been checking the baby regularly and Brighde knew her little girl was developing well. Julie would show her the images on the screen but Brighde always had to battle to avoid thinking about the baby Julie *wasn't* showing her. Her little boy.

Where there had been two babies to keep an eye on, now there was only one. Where there had been two heartbeats there was now only one and Brighde wasn't feeling up to coping with that today. Not straight after her conversation with Sarah, which had filled her head with thoughts of Xavier.

'I'm not here to do an ultrasound,' Julie replied, pulling a letter from the pocket of her white hospital coat. 'I have the results of your amniocentesis.'

'Oh.' Brighde could feel sweat gathering on her upper lip.

This was it. She would no longer be able to put things off. No longer be able to hide behind the excuse that she didn't have all the facts. She was about to find out, once and for all, just exactly what she was dealing with.

'Do you want me to look at the results first or would you like to do it?' Julie asked.

Brighde shook her head. 'You do it,' she replied. She knew she wouldn't be able to even open the envelope. Her hands were shaking and she was terrified of what she might find. No, it was much better to be told the results. She couldn't bear to have to read it for herself.

'Do you want to wait for Xavier?' Julie asked.

Did she? She wasn't sure.

No. It was better to get this over and done with quickly, like pulling off a sticking plaster. She didn't want to delay the inevitable and this way there would be time then for her to digest the information before she would have to share it with anyone else.

She shook her head. 'No. I'll tell him later.' Once she'd had time to compose herself, if necessary.

She reached for Sarah's hand and held it tight as she closed her eyes. 'Okay.'

She could hear the rustle of paper as Julie opened the envelope and pulled out the contents. Brighde held her breath and kept her eyes closed.

'Two tests,' she heard Julie say. 'Both negative.'

She hadn't passed on the defective gene. She

felt the tears well up as reality took hold. Both her babies would have been fine. If they'd both survived. But she'd already lost one.

Sarah was by her side before the sadness could overcome her. She wrapped her arms around Brighde, providing comfort. 'It's okay. You'll have a healthy child who will have every chance of living a long life,' she said, understanding what was going through Brighde's mind while reminding her of what was important.

Everything she'd been worried about hadn't come to pass. She had much to be grateful for. She would have a healthy baby. She needed to be strong and focused now. She could still mourn her loss but her daughter deserved all her attention now.

It was hard to believe. She was going to be a mother and Xavier would get the child he wanted. Their daughter.

Xavier.

'Shall I get him?' Sarah asked.

'Get who?'

'Xavier,' came Sarah's reply and Brighde realised that she'd spoken his name out loud.

She nodded. He deserved to know the outcome.

She had no reason to delay. They would have to work out their arrangements. They needed to have a discussion about what would happen next.

Brighde caught her breath when Xavier walked into the room. She hadn't seen him for four days but it felt like weeks and she'd almost forgotten how gorgeous he was. His familiar scent of honey and pear followed him in, wrapping around her. God, she'd missed him.

He looked divine but he also looked miserable.

She'd done that to him and she felt terrible. This separation had all been her fault. She knew she had been unfair. She couldn't put all the blame on him but it had been easier to shut him out than to see him. Seeing him just reminded her of what she'd lost.

But she hadn't lost everything—she was going to have a healthy baby—but her behaviour meant that she had lost more than she needed to. She'd lost one baby and pushed Xavier away. Xavier who, just possibly, might have been the love of her life.

But she was too proud to admit that.

'Sarah said you wanted to see me?' He looked utterly dejected. She wanted to put a smile back on his face and she hoped her news would do that. She hoped she hadn't made such a mess of things that she couldn't fix it. She hoped she hadn't left it too late.

She nodded. All the anger she'd felt had dissipated and now she was just sad that that things hadn't worked out. Tears welled in her eyes but she fought them back. This wasn't a time for tears. Crying would be self-indulgent. She owed Xavier an explanation. She owed him the truth. There would be time for tears later.

He took a step closer. 'What's happened?' he asked. Had he seen the tears in her eyes?

'Nothing,' she replied as the tears spilled from her lashes; triggered by the concern in his voice, she couldn't hold them back.

'Shh.' He was by the bed now. He sat down and took her in his arms. She closed her eyes and leant against him as he stroked her hair. 'It's okay. I'm here.'

He kissed her forehead and waited for her to calm down. Waited for her tears to subside. She sniffed as she got her emotions under control.

'Are you sure everything's okay?' he asked as he passed her a tissue.

She nodded again and took the tissue from him, aware that she was still clutching the piece of paper that Julie had left with her.

'I'm glad you asked for me,' he said as she blew her nose. 'There are some things I need to tell you.'

Brighde steeled herself for bad news. She couldn't believe that today could only bring good news. That wasn't how her life worked. Good news was always followed by bad.

'I need to talk to you,' he continued. 'I've had

some time to think since you banished me.' He put a finger on her lips as she opened her mouth to protest. 'It's okay, I probably deserved it. I realise that I might have made too much of an issue about your pregnancy and the babies and not enough about you. This isn't just about the baby. I want the whole deal. The baby and you.'

'Xavier, we've discussed this. You don't have to make promises just to ensure you see your daughter. I'm not going to cut you out of her life.'

'That's not what I'm doing. I know I didn't give your feelings, your needs priority. I didn't give *you* priority. I was doing exactly what my ex-girlfriend accused me of, putting everything else ahead of a relationship. My work, the decisions about our children, and forgetting about you and what you need. I made a mistake. One I'd like to rectify if you'll give me a chance. I don't want to lose you. You're too important to me. I want you in my life, not because you are the mother of my child but because I love you.'

'You love me?'

'I love you and I want to share my life with you. Not co-parenting. I want it all. I want us to have a future together, a family together.

'You know, you were right, this wasn't how I would have planned to have a family, but I'm glad it's you. You captivated me from the moment I first saw you and when I learned you were pregnant I could imagine us as a family, but now, even more than that, I can imagine us as a couple. You are strong, brave, honest and beautiful and I don't want to think of my life without you in it. Things happen for a reason and I think we were supposed to meet.

'You challenge me, you can be stubborn and opinionated but, according to my sisters, I need that, and according to me I need you. And I'd like you to give me a chance. To see if there's any way you could love me too. We've got four months to ourselves. To spend some time together. You might even decide you like dating me. And then we can work out what is best for us as well as for the baby. I promise not to men-tion marriage again, not until you're ready, but I want us to do this together. What do you think?'

'I like the sound of that.' Brighde smiled, almost afraid to believe this was really happening. 'I'm sorry I shut you out.'

'It's okay. I know you were scared. There were so many things we couldn't control but I meant it when I told you I had no intention of going anywhere. I know you felt alone and I was trying to make sure you knew I would be there for you, but I should have told you sooner how I felt. I'm not about to walk away from the best thing that's ever happened to me. And, just to be clear, I'm talking about you. Our baby is the icing on the cake. I know you are reluctant to make any commitments until you have the test results back but I wanted you to know how I feel *before* then. I can be patient, despite what my sisters might tell you. I can give you the time and space you need, but it was important to me to tell you how I feel. I love you and I want to be a part of your life. Regardless of what happens with this pregnancy.'

'We need to talk about that. That's why I needed to see you. I need to speak to you about the baby.' She held up the piece of paper. 'I got the amnio results back just now.'

'Oh.' That worried look was back in his eyes but this time Brighde knew she could erase it. He loved her and she had a chance of getting everything she wanted. They both did. 'And?' he asked.

Brighde grinned. 'She's fine. She tested negative.'

'Everything is okay?'

She nodded.

'Really? You're certain?'

She handed him the results and waited while he scanned the page.

His answering smile was enough for her. More than enough. But he followed it with a kiss. A lingering kiss on her lips that brought her back to life. He loved her. His kiss was the water for her damaged heart and it swelled with love for him as his kiss nourished her.

'So, what do you think?'

'Do you really love me?'

'I do.'

She didn't think she would ever get tired of hearing that. 'I find it hard to believe I can get good news and to have two lots in one day, it's almost too much.'

'Every day can be a good day if we are together.'

'I can't believe I almost blew my one chance at my own happily ever after.'

'You didn't blow it. I'm right here and here I intend to stay, if you'll have me. Do you think there's room for me in your life?'

'Yes,' she said as her smile threatened to split her face in two. 'Definitely.'

'What do you think of this one?' Xavier asked as he pushed a pram back and forth on the shop floor. 'We can add a toddler seat to it later.'

Brighde didn't mind which pram they got; she just wished he'd hurry up and choose one. Her back was aching and she wanted to get home and put her feet up. She knew they had to choose a pram, and a bassinette of some description, as they were running out of time to get organised. She was booked in for a Caesarean section next week, but she was having trouble concentrating. She rubbed her stomach as a ripple of pain ran across her abdomen.

'Are you okay?'

'I think I need to sit down,' she replied as a second spasm gripped her, hard and fast and low in her belly. She gasped as the pain made her catch her breath. That was way too close to the first one.

'Was that a contraction?' She could hear the concern in Xavier's voice. She didn't want him to worry. She needed him to keep her calm.

'I'm not sure,' she said, but what she really meant was, *It's too soon. I'm not ready to have a baby.*

And then Xavier was beside her. Right where she needed him to be. He took charge, took control, took care of her and she felt her panic ease. As long as he was beside her she would be okay.

* * *

'Congratulations. She is perfect,' Julie said as she handed Brighde her daughter.

She was early and tiny but she was perfect. Ten fingers, ten toes and downy blonde hair. She grasped Brighde's finger and looked up at her with blue-grey eyes.

'Hello, Bessie.' She and Xavier had agreed to name her after Brighde's mum. It was the perfect name; she was a miniature version of her grandmother.

'You did it.' Xavier leant over and kissed her forehead.

Brighde lifted her face, meeting his lips with hers. 'We did it.' She smiled. 'Together.'

'Xavier?' Julie interrupted. Xavier straightened up and Brighde held her breath as Julie passed her husband a second blanket-wrapped baby. Their son.

'Can I hold him?' she asked.

The midwife took Bess. 'I'll clean her and do her name tags,' she said as Xavier laid their baby boy on Brighde's chest.

'Hello, my darling.' He was exceptionally small, still the size he had been at eighteen weeks, but he was recognisable as a tiny person. Brighde's eyes filled with tears but she refused to be sad. Not today.

She held him for a long time but her arms longed to hold Bess too.

'There's a cuddle cot in here,' Xavier told her. 'Would you like to use that and then you can say goodbye when you are ready?' Had he seen the longing in her eyes? The dilemma she was facing? She wasn't ready to say goodbye but she needed to cuddle Bess. Her arms needed to hold her daughter.

She nodded. The refrigerated bassinette was the perfect solution. She could keep her son with her until they were ready to let go.

Xavier lifted him from her arms and the midwife returned Bess to her.

'Are you okay?' he asked.

'Yes.' She had Xavier beside her and their daughter. She had more than she'd ever thought possible. 'I am.' She smiled at the father of her children. 'I have everything I need.'

'There's one more thing I need,' Xavier told her as he put their son into the chilled bassinette and wheeled it closer to Brighde. 'I need us to be a proper family. I love you and I want to be your husband. I want to give you commitment and security and love. I want the world to know we are a family. Will you marry me?'

EPILOGUE

BRIGHDE STOOD AT the end of the aisle and took a minute or two to savour the moment. She'd never dared to dream that she would have this day—a wedding of her own—and she wanted to be able to remember every second. She only intended to do this once.

'Are you ready?'

She turned to her brother. He stood beside her, strong and steady, waiting patiently to walk her down the aisle. For so long it had been just the two of them but now Nick had a wife and baby of his own and today it was her turn to extend the family just a little more.

She nodded and tucked her arm through Nick's as the organist started to play. She was vaguely aware of the guests swivelling in their seats as they turned to watch her make her entrance but she only had eyes for Xavier.

He was waiting for her at the altar. Her stomach did a little flip as he met her gaze with his come-to-bed eyes. She hoped she never got used to the effect he had on her whenever she saw him.

She kept her eyes on him as she walked down the aisle. He was wearing the dark navy suit he'd worn on the night they'd met. His hair was a little shorter but still had the wildness in the curl and his thighs were just as lean and powerful under the fabric, his shoulders just as broad. The suit wasn't necessarily traditional wedding attire but Brighde suspected she'd fallen in love with Xavier on that very first night and she wanted a little reminder of that evening. Although, she conceded, the suit was probably unnecessary as Xavier held another, far more precious reminder in his arms. Their four-month-old daughter, Bess.

Nick put Brighde's hand into Xavier's and

took his niece, leaving Brighde and Xavier alone at the front of the church.

Xavier squeezed her hand and smiled. 'You look beautiful.'

Brighde got lost in his eyes and, despite her plan of memorising every minute, she scarcely heard a word the priest said. All she could focus on was Xavier, the love of her life, and the fact that they were about to officially become a family.

'I now pronounce you husband and wife.'

Brighde tuned back in as the priest said the words she'd been waiting to hear.

'You may kiss the bride.'

Xavier turned to her. He was grinning from ear to ear as he cupped her face in one hand and tilted her head towards him before bending to kiss her.

She closed her eyes as his lips found hers. She reached for him, her fingers curling around the back of his neck, holding him to her, never wanting to let him go as they sealed their commitment to each other.

'And now, if the godparents could bring Bess up to join us,' the priest invited as Xavier and Brighde finally broke their kiss.

Today was going to be a double celebration. While family and friends were already gathered, Brighde felt it was the perfect time to christen Bess as well. Sarah carried Bess to the baptismal font, her maid of honour duties temporarily suspended as she, along with Xavier's sister Mary and her husband, took on their responsibilities as godparents.

'Brighde and Xavier, what name have you given your child?'

'Elizabeth Marie O'Donnell.'

Bess had been named after both her grandmothers, although she remained the spitting image of Brighde's mum. Brighde thought about the son they'd lost. He was a constant presence in her subconscious and she knew she'd never forget him. Each milestone Bess marked would be another reminder but the pain and sorrow Brighde felt was lessening with time. She had a lot to be thankful for and plenty to look forward to.

Mary held Bess above the font as the priest continued the proceedings. 'Elizabeth Marie, I baptise you in the name of the Father,' he said as he poured warm water over her blonde curls, 'and of the Son—' Brighde waited for the tears to start but Bess was quiet until the second wetting '—and of the Holy Spirit.'

She started crying in earnest now, reaching her chubby little hands out to her father as Mary lifted her from the font. She settled the moment she was in Xavier's arms. She was such a daddy's girl but Brighde could understand why. She loved him just as fiercely and felt just as safe and secure when she was in his arms.

She smiled as she looked at her family. It was a perfect day, surrounded by everyone she loved, and she couldn't ask for anything more.

* * * * *